Short n Scary Stories Publication
This Book is a mix of fiction and true scary stories written by proficient authors from all around the globe. Characters, places, etc. may or may not be author's imagination, any resemblance to events or places are coincidental.

Copyright 2015, Short n Scary Stories
All rights are reserved for printed publication or reproduction of any other form.

Book Design by Eyebridge Soft Solutions Pvt. Ltd

# # #

AF365702

Introduction

It's been almost 5 years since we started **ShortnScary Stories**, with only one objective in our mind that this website should become a platform to read stories which none of us have never heard or read before. We along with the great help of Eyebridge team made this idea into a surprisingly scary reality. Amazingly this site picked up very well, and the kind of growth which we saw was something we never imagined. Within a year's time, we became one of the most popular sites of our genre.

Since inception, we have received more than 5000 stories with a network of about 20000 contributors. It has been a fascinating journey altogether, and this year "2015" is even better, we recently launched our SnS Mobile App and are now launching our first book **"Endless Darkness - 26 Hand Picked Horror Stories"**.

The Book

Endless Darkness is a tribute to all the contributors, authors and my fellow teammates for bringing more blackness into our temple. This book is a symbol in itself that some unknown people from different backgrounds & locations can come together to create something so unique that you just simply feel good about it. I'm thankful to all the published authors for giving us pieces of their evil minds. This book contains 26 Stories written by 19 authors. These 26 stories have been selected out of 5000 stories submitted on ShortnScary Stories in past five years.

I read this book quite a lot of times, and the kind of depth in these different genres of Horror stories made me thrilled and wondered every time I read it. These short stories are going to leave an impact on your mind, so consider that as a warning before you read further.

The Authors

We didn't select any author by their name, fame or anything attached to their existence. Only criteria were their stories. Our authors are from all over the globe, age ranging from Teens to Seventies. We took a lot of care while selecting the final set of stories. We have a rating system and popularity meter for all the stories on our website, and the data is based on reader's feedback, which has 75% weight in the overall score. 25% selection weight has been given to critic scores. We had to select only 26 stories out of 5000 original stories, so selection process was quite tricky for us. We are proud of all the 19 published authors but would like to say that the work which has not been published is also very special.

Acknowledgement

I think this hobby of writing and reading scary stories was little unorthodox, and sometimes people find it creepy to see me running a Scary Stories website, and they ask why only scary? It's always little difficult to explain to such people. But lucky for me I have some encouraging individuals who helped us in this journey. I would like to thank my Dear friends Mr. Vivek Rathore, Mr. Jaideep Chauhan and Ms. Neetika, who have been part of this whole concept from the beginning.

I want to thank my parents Mr. R.K. Gupta and Mrs. Santosh Gupta, my brother and his wife Mr. Raghav Gupta & Mrs. Shiefa Gupta for all their support.

Finally, I would like to mention my year old beautiful daughter Ms. Saamya and my amazing wife Mrs. Ruhani Gupta, who have been a continuous inspiration throughout my life and its misadventures.

Jagrit Gupta
Founder & Editor
Short n Scary Stories

Table of Content

The Hole
by Peter Hartke

I understand why it was there. I mean, I'm not stupid. It was there for a convenience. It made perfect sense, the floor of the bathroom closet sat right over the laundry room. So yes, it made sense to put in a laundry chute.

The part I wonder about is why it became to be known as, "The Hole," and why that name stuck.

Just the name, "The Hole" had an ominous sound to it. You couldn't ever picture something called "The Hole" to be a good place. It was like the word pit, or the word dungeon. These words have their own weight, their own mood, their own image that they evoke in your brain. Pictures connected and entwined with them in our mind's eye.

It's one of the things you have to love about the English language, not just the meaning of a word, but the imagery it brings to mind.

It's powerful.

So how such a word, a dark word if you would, became associated with our laundry chute I can not understand.

I remember the day my father cut the opening. He had his tool belt out, so you knew right away this was serious work, not just some lame repair. Also there were power tools, always a good sign.

My brother Frankie, he was ten at the time, two years older than I am. He was always Dad's helper, there to hand him tools and learning how to change the electric saw blade, draw chalk lines and how to make relief cuts. Cool, useful stuff like that, and he loved learning it.
Me?

Me, I was content to watch, I didn't seem to have any natural talent with tools, nor did I have the drive or desire to learn that my brother did. So I watched, watched Dad as he marked out the space, using his chalk line, its silver body and wind up handle always made me long to go fishing.

I watched as he took his drill, lining it up in one corner and drilling down and into the floor wood chips flying out in a small geyser. My baby sister, Ruthie, wondered by at that moment, asking her ever popular question "watz zat?" as she watched dad handle the drill.

Ruthie was only four, and a bit of a handful. Mom said she kept her busier than a box full of monkeys, a thought that never failed to make me laugh. She was in the phase where everything she saw or was told brought one of two questions from her, "why?" or "wazzat?"

Dad just ignored her, he was busy showing Frankie how he was going to make the cut, and promising to maybe let him run the saw a little. Mom stopped by to "check progress" she said, but also to gather Ruth before she pestered dad to much. "Come on chickie" She said to Ruth, come help me in the kitchen.

Ruth answered with a predictable "Why" but took mom's hand and let herself be lead away. Dad was setting the saw up now, and as promised he would let Frank run it. He placed the saw blade in the hole he drilled and started cutting, explaining to Frank as he went.

"See.. see Frankie? You want to stay just inside of the line. Use it as a guide, but leave the line. Understand?" Frank nodded, his eyes bright and excited, he looked with fascination at the saw. "Yeah Dad. I can do it."

I watched him make most of the rest of the cut, dad encouraging him all the way. "That's it, nice and slow. Let the saw do the work, don't push it, nice and easy. You're doing great!"

It had gotten a little boring for me by then, so I left all the action and headed down into the basement (basement, not cellar. See, cellar is a dark word too. Evil dark holes cellars are.) to watch some TV.

The weekend channel line up was always filled with the old horror movies back in those days. Creature double feature, Dr. Shock, all brought you guaranteed chills through the long days of summer when it was to hot to be outside unless it was to go in the pool.

By the time mom called us for dinner, most of the construction was over. They were busy laying molding along the edges of the newly made opening as mom trying to convince them they could finish after they ate, "come on, food is getting cold."

After dinner, after the last piece of molding was put in place, with the whole family gathered around. Dad christened the new chute, "John," he said to me, "Go grab some of your dirty clothes and throw them down the hole."

I did as asked, and we all watched and clapped as my dirty shirt and pants disappeared from view, swallowed by "The Hole"

That was apparently all the excitement my family could stand for the evening, and we soon split up to do our own thing.

Ok, I know I have this obsession with words and language. Growing up I read voraciously, starting with comic books but quickly developing an appetite for fiction. Especially horror fiction.

All of this reading just feed into my love of language, and the pictures you could draw with just words, The feelings words could make you feel. How real words could make you feel.

Sticks and stones may break my bones, but words can never hurt me? I don't believe that. The paper is filled with stories of young people, boys and girls, ending their life because of the pain of words. Words of torment heard every day. Wrists slashed and overdoses, even hangings due to words like fat, stupid, dyke, fag.

Words can't hurt you? Look into these kids dead lifeless eyes, then tell me words don't have power.

I laid in bed that night, thinking about the day, replaying parts like a private movie in my head as I waited for sleep to come. My mind seized on the word hole. Turning it over in my mind and examining it like an archaeologist might study a rare artifact.

Hole. What did the word project to me, what images did it hold. The first thought I had was of solitary confinement in a prison. A dark, damp, cold place that they would put prisoners who would or could not conform. ("Let's see if a week in 'The Hole' doesn't cure that attitude" Johnny, the prison guard said with a sneer.)

The second image that the word brought to mind was one of a well. A deep dark hole, surrounded by bricks in a circular pattern on the ground around the opening. Not a wishing well, the well in my mind was flat against the ground it sat on, a dangerous thing waiting to devour any small children or animals that unluckily stopped to investigate its opening.

Things came out of holes. Dark things. Nasty, slimy things. They hid in holes during the day, unable to stand the touch of sunlight against their pallid skin. They preferred to stay in the shadows, even at night. They hid in the places of nightmares.

As these thoughts spun out in my mind, I realized there was pressure in my bladder, and I better go "drain the monster". A term Frankie had just taught me and I couldn't help but find it hilarious!
My room was right across the hall from the bathroom. The new improved bathroom, now home to "The Hole".

The bathroom had a design flaw. The door to the closest, was a bifold, it split in the middle when opened and the two halves drew next to each other thanks to a track along the top.

The flaw was, if the doors were not perfectly closed, if they were not flush with each other, the bathroom door would hit them, and you couldn't close the door.

The bathroom door was closed when I walked across the hall, and I pushed it open, ready for sleep now, my head heavy. When the door opened, it struck the doors of the closet. The noise and the unexpected, though only momentary resistance made me jump slightly in the dark hallway.

As I walked into the room, I looked at the doors, pushing them fully closed. Odd I thought, that someone left it opened and was able to close the door. I stood at the toilet (I was a big boy now and didn't need the stairs that still sat next to the tub.) and started peeing when I heard a noise. A noise from the closet.

It was an odd noise, and to this day, I can't swear I really heard it, but at the moment, I did. It was a wet, squishy sound, reminding me of the sound that my sneakers made when we went to the bay, and walked in the mud along the shores to set out minnow traps. If you weren't careful the thick mud would steal your shoe right off of your foot. That mud, the shoe sucking mud, made the same squishy sound that I heard in the closet.

My eyes went to the closet door, and I thought I saw it tremble, as if trying to open. This I am less sure of than hearing the sound though, so I don't blame you for not believing.
I cut off my urine and stood for a full two minutes at least straining my ears and listening, my eyes never leaving the door, every nerve in my body now awake and singing.

Nothing. It's nothing stupid I scolded myself as I finished my business, but keeping my eyes on the door as the monster finished being drained. I felt a little stupid and like a baby, a scaredy-cat, I wouldn't tell Frankie about this. He would just tease me. Even with all that said, after I flushed and washed my hands, I gave the closet door a wide berth when as I exited and closed the bathroom door firmly behind me before returning to bed.

Sleep came slowly as images of slow, slimy monsters filled my imagination. Each one making that awful wet sucking sound as they moved. Gelatinous goo dripped from each razor sharp claw and hit the floor with a wet plopping sound like dropping a sponge full of water on the ground.

Over the next few days, my unease at the new addition to the bathroom had me avoid going in there unless I absolutely had to. I even carried my laundry down the steps and into the laundry room rather than open the closet door which now contained "The Hole"

I remember standing in the laundry room, staring up at the square opening cut into the plywood above. From here, it wasn't as scary. From below, it was a chute, not a hole. My mind worked hard, trying to convince myself I was just being silly, anything that came out of "The Hole" would have to start its journey here, in the basement.

And there just wasn't anything there.

I wish I could tell you that the sane, rational, part of my mind easily convinced the darker, more base, spiritual part (my soul perhaps?) of the fact that no monster in the basement meant no monster in the cute, no monster in the closet, no monster coming up from "The Hole".
The sane me was winning, and I was starting to feel better as I went up the stairs until my dark side asked, "How do you know a hole always ends in the same place. When you are above, staring down into the inky blackness of the abyss, how can you be sure where you will end up when you can't see the bottom".

I suppose that is what faith is, knowing anything that went into the hole, would find its way safely to the laundry basket that sat next to the washer.
Only, what if that wasn't true. What if the hole, the darkness, could somehow read the sacrifice it was offered, and then decide where this item should go.

I was much older when I first read Nietzsche's quote on the abyss, "And if you gaze long enough into an abyss, the abyss will gaze back into you".

When I first heard the quote, it stopped my heart for a moment, because it perfectly described my thoughts at that time. When I peer into the dark, I open myself up to the dark. When I step into the dark, I place myself at its mercy.

Following this bizarre yet compelling logic, (I was only eight, please remember!) if the darkness read you, and could alter the destination of those people or objects that entered it based on what it learned from that reading. Then it is also possible it could spew forth from its depths creatures or items from other places, dark places where monsters live.

This idea, this thought, made me ice to my core in fear. The possibilities were horrifying. My imagination ran wild, as it will do when you are still that young, and then another thought crept in.

The name. The name we gave our laundry chute. Could it be possible, when my father named our man made abyss, giving it a dark word as a name, could that have affected the type of darkness our hole was filled with? Could an object named with a dark word call forth a demon or it's like? Were words that powerful?

These were the thoughts I was still contemplating when I was laying in my bed that night. I think I slept earlier, right after coming to bed, but now I was awake and had been for maybe an hour.

It was coming up at 3 AM according to our trusted clock radio. The house was quite. I heard the TV go off in mom and dad's room about a half hour ago and nothing until Frankie got up to use the bathroom.

I listened as he opened our door, padded across the hall and opened the bathroom door, and heard it shut behind him. I was starting to drift off when I hear him open the bathroom door, then our door, then climb back into bed.

I was mostly asleep, drifting in between world of dreams and reality, when two things happened almost simultaneously that brought me fully awake. I still can't tell which happened first, even after wracking my brain for all these years.

What I believe came first was the realization that I hadn't heard the bathroom door close when Frankie came back to bed. The second was a noise. A creak from the hallway. The creak of the floorboard that sat just past the bathroom and down the small hallway going towards my parent's room and also towards Ruthie's.

I knew the sound well, like I knew just about all of the sounds this old house made. I knew where to step to avoid the noisy board also. Stealth learned from countless hide and seek games with my brother and our friends.

That sound, that creak, meant someone was in the hall. Someone was walking down the hall and across the noisy floor board with its asthmatic sounding reee Hhheee squeal.

I strained my ears trying to hear any follow up sounds, my stomach already practicing origami as it twisted and turned on itself, a low growing noise of protest coming from my gut.

I thought I heard something, that squelching sound, and I slowly got out of bed and went to the door. Cracking it open slowly, I could see the bathroom door standing wide open, and behind it, the closet door was also open.

Then I knew I heard a sound. The sound. From down the hall towards my parents room, that wet sound from my nightmares. It wasn't at my parents door though, it was at Ruthie's.

My horror grew deeper as I heard her soft, sweet, little voice "waz zat?"
I heard the monster reply in a wet garbled sound that made me think of black, damp, rotting things you find under rocks. I could make no sense of the words though, I couldn't tell what it was trying to say.

Ruthie could, apparently, as I heard her reply, "why?"

More dark slurping noises, and then again, her reply. A rare one, words she only said when she was excited about what you had offered.

"OK"

I was frozen to the spot. I was only eight years old for christ's sake, how was I supposed to stop a monster. I was only eight!

So I stood there as I heard the monster from the hole coming down the hall with my baby sister.

I often think... if I acted quicker, come into the hall sooner, blocked his way somehow... Maybe.. maybe Ruthie would still be alive.
But I didn't.
I didn't move, couldn't move, as I heard the floorboard creak again and saw a large shadow slipping along the wall. Trailing behind it was my sister, Ruthie, looking like she hadn't a care in the world. Her tiny hand clasp in this monster's hideous claw.

It wasn't until the monster entered the bathroom, Ruthie happily following, that I started screaming. Screaming at the top of my lungs. "You let go of my sister!" I shrieked, "Let her go!"

The monster swept into the bathroom, dragging my sister behind him, for the first time her face showing confusion. "John?" she squeaked before being drug into the room.

I heard my father's feet hit the floor in their bedroom, and mom's worried cry of "What is it?", but it was that look on my sister's face that finally got my legs moving. I heard Frank call out as I flung the door open, "What's going on?" but I ignored him as I ran as fast as I could to the bathroom.
As I skidded to a stop in front of the open closet door, I got my first good look at the monster. Its face was little more than a skull. What flesh was left was infested with maggots and shiny black beetles that crawled along the surface.

It smelled of rotting leaves and its bright black beetle eyes landed on me and it gave an evil hiss. Ruthie was now wrapped in its arms and her face showed real fear. "Johnny!" she screamed, reaching out to me as the monster sank into the hole, dragging my sister with it.

I didn't think, there wasn't any time. I dove for the hole, head first like I was going into a pool. My head and shoulders slipped easily into the hole but I was stopped short when something grabbed my ankle.

It was my father. He had come into the room just as I was diving, and he caught me by the ankle as I went into the hole. I heard him yell something, but his words were like a million miles away.

I hung down in the hole, my hips just past the edge, my father holding me in place by my leg. What I saw... well.. it wasn't my basement. The hole continued down maybe another ten feet, its edges widening as it went. The walls were black and slimy, smelling of rot.

I could see the monster, still dragging my sister along, her screams of terror broken up by her sobbing, her free hand reaching back to me for help.

It wasn't all I saw though.
There were many monsters, hundreds of them it seemed. They climbed and scurried along the walls of the hole like insects, reaching for me with their terrible sharp claws.

My father hauled me out of the hole by my leg, dragging me into the bathroom floor and turning on the light.

"John! What the hell are..."

But I cut him off, screaming "no!"
I crawled back to the edge of the hole, peering in, looking into the darkness.

Except it wasn't dark. The light from the bathroom spilled in the hole, and down below, maybe ten feet away, I saw the laundry basket that caught the dirty clothes.

I was in shock then. Or that's what they told me later, when I came back, came back to being in my head.

They wanted to know what happened, what happened to Ruthie, where was she.

So I told them. I told them everything I saw as I am telling you now. I told them of the monster, of the darkness of the hole, and the things that lived in there. The monster who took Ruthie lived in the darkness, and now Ruthie did too.

I saw lots of doctors after that. Looked at endless ink blots and talked about everything from my parents to if I ever had any sexual thoughts. (I giggled the first time I was asked this. It felt good. It was the only real laugh I had since all this happened.)
They asked, and I told them the same story.
Over and over again.

I didn't realize till much later that they thought I did it. That I did something to Ruthie. I even saw it in my mother's eyes.

One night she broke down in the hospital room I had been confined to since that night. "Please John" she sobbed, dropping to her knees before me. Her fingers wrapped and clutching at the gown I wore. "Please tell me, what did you do to Ruthie. What did you do to my baby girl!"

Her sobs were hysterical and she was scaring me, my father drug her off me and wrestled her into the hall, slamming the door closed with his foot. But I still heard her, heard her scream that I had taken her little girl from her.

They stopped visiting after that. It's been five years now since I last saw them. Even the doctors seem to have lost interest. They stopped asking me questions long ago.
All they do now is adjust my medications once every few months, that's it, otherwise I just sit in my room, like a medicated zombie.
But not a night passes, that when I am drifting off to sleep, that I hear those words.

"Waz zat"
And now I know.

# # #

Peter Hartke
Peter Lives in a quiet town with his wife Tiffanna and their three dogs who are more like their kids.

Don't Touch The Darkness
*by **P.L. DuPeé***

Working at a morgue wasn't Victor's favorite thing to do, especially on a Saturday night. His dream was to become a doctor and this was the only opportunity to gain experience that was available. Working at a hospital would have been ideal, but he was only a college freshman and all of the good jobs and internships went to seniors and graduates.

The job was kind of boring, he didn't get to handle the bodies or assist in the autopsies, he just processed forms. Occasionally he got to put the toe tags on the bodies and push them into the freezers. Sometimes he would prep and clean the coroner's work area before he did an autopsy, but he mostly just entered data into the computer and verified that all of the proper forms in the coroner's report were filled out and signed.

Victor would usually work a late night shift and was alone for most of the evening. Being alone in that building scared him sometimes. He wasn't afraid of the dead, like most people were. It was the silence that got to him. It was always really quiet, except for the low hum of the fluorescent light bulbs and the clicking of the computer keys. It was hard to concentrate on his work because of the silence. The building would produce many unknown noises and every little sound was amplified one hundred times.

The one perk of the job was the files, even though he would never tell anyone that. Each person's file contained all of the gory details about their cause of death. Sometimes he would pull the bodies out of their refrigerated drawers and examine them while he read their files.

Victor sat as his desk and lazily flipped through a folder. It was an old woman who died of a stroke. It was one of the boring files with nothing interesting in it. He had about 8 files to go through before he could go home, but was in no real hurry. The night before, he had stayed out late partying and drinking and was still feeling the effects.
The coroner, Joe, was a man in his sixties with a full head of gray hair. He rushed across the room, hastily putting on his coat. He didn't usually leave this early, it was only ten thirty. "You gonna be alright here tonight?", asked Joe. "You ask me that every time", Victor replied.

"Sorry about leaving you alone with so much work, but I just remembered that I had to pick up my daughter and grandson from the airport. When you get my age, you tend to forget things now and again", said Joe. They shared a laugh as Joe put his jacket on. Joe continued, "Just do what you can and I'll finish the rest in the morning." Victor waved goodbye and returned to the open folder, eager to move on to the next one. Joe's dress shoes clicked down the hallway, growing fainter with each step until they were no longer audible.

He was relieved to be done with the stroke lady and eagerly pulled the next folder from the stack. His eyes widened with excitement. This folder contained a girl named Robin and the cause of death was suicide by overdose. She was his age, just twenty years old. She was very pretty and he stared at her picture for several minutes. He wondered why such a pretty girl would want to kill herself? What could have been so bad in her life? He would normally wait until later in the evening to look at the bodies, but he couldn't wait, not this time.

Victor made his way into the room where the bodies were kept and slid her out of the cold metal drawer. She lay there, fully nude and was just as pretty in person. She didn't look like she was dead, more like she was sleeping. The bodies normally turned gray after being dead for several hours, but she was still tan and very much alive looking. He stared at her naked body, eyes investigating every detail. He swallowed hard and reached his hand out to touch her breast, they were perfect, even in death. He was hesitant and his hand trembled slightly as it drew closer. He knew he wasn't supposed to do this, but it wasn't like she was gonna tell on him. Her skin was smooth and felt like cold leather. He nervously looked at the door several times to make sure no one was watching him. His hand glided down the length of her body, across her breast, down her stomach, along her thigh, then back up. He had never touched a girl this pretty and moved slowly, admiring every contour. He didn't know why he was touching her or why he liked it so much, but it didn't let that stop him. He ran his finger over her pouty lips, and pink lipstick smeared on his finger. He brought it to his mouth and tasted it. To his surprise, he had an erection and after some mental debate, he used his free hand to unzip his zipper. He was planning on relieving himself. As his unoccupied hand made its way back to her breast, he heard his name whispered, "Victor". He quickly turned to the door, certain he had been caught, but no one was there. He turned back around to find the girl's eyes open and fixed on him, "Please don't do this to me", she whispered. He tripped and fell backwards, his head and back hit the wall on his way to the ground. He grabbed his head in pain and rolled around on the tile floor, cradling it as he groaned. As he touched the back of his head, his hands came away with no blood. A chain of obscenities escaped him as he sat there. He looked up at Robin's corpse, waiting for her to move, but she remained lifeless. The longer he stared, the more he felt like an idiot. A nervous laugh escaped him and he felt that he deserved to be scared for what he was doing.

Victor had enough excitement for the night and returned to his desk. He couldn't look at her file anymore, so he moved on to the next one: A black kid in his mid-twenties, two gunshots to the chest. One bullet punctured his lung, the other went through and hit his spine. Victor cringed at the thought and wondered what the wounds looked like. He would have normally had a look at this body, but because of what just happened, he decided to stick to the files.

The long, slow whine of an unlubricated door hinge poured through the building. Victor turned towards the sound, still and attentive, waiting for the source to reveal itself. Maybe Joe forgot something and came back to get it. Victor hoped this was the answer, because strange sounds bothered him more than the silence. The click clack sound of hard bottom shoes made their way down the long entrance hallway. Victor relaxed at the sound and returned to the file. The footsteps made their way, step by step, down the hallway and into the main room. Without turning Victor said, "Forgot something else, huh?" Silence filled the room once again. He swiveled around in his chair, smile still on his face and found that he was alone. The smile quickly melted away. He ran out of the room into the hallway and it was empty. The hallway was about thirty yards straight to the exit and no one was there. Victor took this as a sign to head home, he had enough creepy stuff for one night. As he gathered his things, he remembered that he didn't push Robin back into the freezer drawer. He strolled into the freezer room and stopped dead in his tracks, Robin was gone. A cold chill ran through Victor's body as he stared at an empty metal slab where the dead body of Robin was supposed to be. Either he had imagined the girl or she wasn't really dead, he wasn't sure which he preferred. Thoughts raced through his brain, searching for a rational explanation. She would have said something if she woke up in a morgue, and he would have heard her, right? The problem was, where was she now?

The best thing to do was call Joe and tell him what happened, leaving out the details about his grope session of course. He wanted to leave so badly, he was scared like never before, so he decided to make the call from the car. He turned all of the lights in the main room off and quickly headed towards the exit. The hallway was lined with four sections of overhead lights and had a switch every fifteen feet to turn off that section. Victor began down the hallway, he clicked the first switch, casting the section behind him into darkness. The feeling of being followed permeated his thoughts, but he didn't look back. He was afraid that if he turned to look, he might actually see something. Second switch, click, more darkness. His pace quickened, third switch, click. Finally he was at the exit and he exhaled a long sigh of relief as he pushed the door open. The cold night air hit his face. As he turned back to switch the final light off, he was surprised to find that the first light in the hallway was on. Maybe in his haste, he failed to push the switch down completely.

Victor made his way back down the hallway, turning on each switch that he passed until he reached the first light switch. He pressed down on the switch, hard, making sure it was off this time. As he approached the second light, the footsteps started again, slowly approaching behind him. Victor looked back into the darkness and saw nothing. He ran anyway, slapping each switch off and turning to make sure the lights in that section were off. When he reached the exit door he paused, staring deep into the black hallway. Free from the confines of the morgue walls, Victor flashed his middle finger towards the dark hall in triumph, then flipped the final light off. His hand plunged into his pocket, expecting to find his car keys. His hands moved from pocket to pocket, searching but coming up empty. When Victor found that Robin was missing, he had been so consumed with the event that he failed to pick up the keys from the table.

He had to venture back into the building that he offered a cocky middle finger to. Victor was afraid to go back inside, but he had no choice. He felt like a child being afraid of the dark and of a that place. It wasn't anything more than a building full of dead people, nothing to be afraid of, right? For several minutes he tried to convince himself that he is being childish. "Just your imagination", he said to himself. Finally he built up the courage and ran full speed down the hall.

He saw the keys as he approached his desk. The sight of them was comforting. The keys sat atop of a folder, and as he drew closer, he could see that the folder was Robin's. He knew that he didn't leave them on top of her folder, in fact he remembered placing her folder on the bottom of the pile. The thought of Robin still being alive came back. Of course, it was the only rational explanation, squeaking doors, lights and strange sounds. She was probably wandering around in the dark looking for help.

Victor returned to the freezer room and hoped he would find Robin, but found something horrible. He couldn't move, standing in shock as he looked across the room at the body laying on the metal slab. The body lying in Robin's place was an old woman, the one that died of a stroke. Was this the body he had been touching. He wiped his hands on his shirt in disgust at the thought. The old woman was the total opposite of Robin; her skin was dry and sagging and her breast looked like socks full of sand. Her face was sunken in and she smelled worse than the other bodies.

Victor almost fainted and leaned against the wall to stop from falling, suddenly the room plunged into darkness. Victor gasped, he was out of breath like someone had punched him in the stomach. He stood still in the dark, listening for any noise or movement, but only heard silence. He shifted his weight and stepped away from the wall, the lights flashed back on. Surprised, he looks around for an explanation and realized that he leaned against the light switch. He felt even more childish than before. He wondered if the night could get any stranger, but before he completed the thought, he got his answer. Across the room, on that same metal slab, was Robin. She lay there just as she had before. He pushed her body back into the freezer and noticed a dark burgundy and purple ring around her neck. He hadn't noticed it before, maybe because he was paying so much attention to her tits.

He grabbed his keys and paused for a moment, staring at the folder. Curiosity got the best of him, he had to check something. In the "Cause of Death" section it read: Strangulation. Somehow the C.O.D. had changed from "Suicide By Overdose" to this. He read more and found that Robin had been raped and strangled to death in a gas station bathroom. He flipped through the pages and stopped on an empty form with the words "Don't Touch Me" written in pink lipstick.

Victor backed away from the desk. He had his keys and curiosity quenched and he wanted out, immediately. He made his way into the hallway and ran right past the light switches without turning them off. Even though the hallway was only about 30 yards, it seemed to stretch for a mile. As he approached the door, the light near the exit shut off. Victor stopped dead in his tracks. The darkness was like a wall and so dark that the exit door couldn't be seen just a few feet behind it. He stared deep into it, deciding what to do next. Maybe he could just rush into it and burst out of the door. It would only be a few steps, he thought. Just as he prepared for takeoff, something in the darkness moved. The onyx silhouette moved just beyond the border of the darkness. His plan seemed more dangerous now that the shadowy figure lurked in front of him. Before he could muster up the courage to charge, the first section of lights went out. He spun to find the same black wall of undulating ink behind him too. He was trapped, sandwiched between unknown dangers. Time was against him, and he anticipated that the entire hallway will submerge into the darkness soon and he didn't wanted to be there when it will happen. Charging the door was the only option. He exploded in a full sprint towards the door, screaming out a battle cry in some ill attempt at intimidation. Victor rushed into the darkness like running back on the goal line and disappeared into it.

Victor instantly felt weightless, like he was falling. He couldn't see, but felt cold and sticky like he was in an ocean of cool honey. Even though he felt like he was weightless, he could barely move his arms and legs. He struggled with all of his strength and only moved a few feet. It wasn't as bad as he expected. At any moment, he would push the door open and be outside. His hand found what felt like the door handle and a sharp pain raced through his hand and up his arm. It felt like something bit him. The same pain happened in his right leg, then his side, then his other arm. He was being bitten over and over by something with a small mouth and pencil like teeth. As he opened his mouth to scream and the dark honey slid into his mouth and throat. He squirmed in pain and tried to move away from the door but could only move a little at a time. Just as he thought he would suffocate, he was spewed from the darkness out onto the hallway floor. He coughed and gagged as he sucked in large gulps of air. Victor crawled down the hall so he was right in the middle of the dark walls. The next closest light near the exit flickered and dimmed. Victor was forced to crawl farther away from the exit to avoid being consumed by the darkness as it swallowed another section of hallway.

A shape emerged from the dark, it was Robin. She stood expressionless and said, "You shouldn't have touched me". He cried out a begging apology to her. He apologized for touching her and for what happened to her and that he didn't deserve this. Nothing happened and Victor was unsure if his apology worked. Minutes went by and nothing happened, she just gazed down at him. Suddenly, the lights above him began to flicker and dim. Victor pressed hard on the light switch in an attempt to overpower it from turning off. The lights dimmed so low that he could barely see. He closed his eyes screaming out in pain as he prepared for the bites to resume once the darkness returned. He continued to scream, but nothing happened. He finally opened his eyes and was alone, pressed against the wall in a brightly lit hallway. The exit was right there in plain sight, no dark wall, no dead girl. He had never been so happy to leave work and briskly headed for the door. Just a few more feet and he would be home free. He imagined the cold night air hitting his skin. As he approached the door, the lights flickered and he immediately made a dash for the exit. The hallway was fully eclipsed and stopped him dead in his tracks. The bytes returned and touched every part of his body. His painful screams were muffled by the thick darkness as the bites increased in intensity.

Victor opened his eyes, he was laying on the ground in front of Robin's body. Confused and not sure where he was, he scanned the room until his memory returned. He must have hit his head pretty hard and blacked out when he thought Robin spoke to him. He laughed out loud, happy to not be devoured by the dark hallway. There was no such thing as ghosts anyway, he should have known better. He stood up and stared at Robin's body again. Even though the bites and darkness were still very present in his mind, he pushed them to the side. All of that was just his conscious manifesting itself in a screwed up dream. He reached his hand out and poked her body with his index finger. She remained still and silent. He gently rested his hand on her, barely making contact with her skin. His eyes left her for a moment to look over his shoulder and when they returned, Robin's eyes were open staring at Victor. He heard one last thing as the room is swallowed by darkness, "I told you not to".

# # #

P.L. DuPeé

P.L. DuPeé is an author from the San Francisco Bay area. He has a passion for all thing related to horror and discovered his love for writing horror while pursuing a Master's degree in Cinema. He specializes in creating stories centered around villains and morally conflicted characters. He aims to turn the typical antagonist into the protagonist by exploring the motivations and desires of the people and creatures we fear and rarely understand. His first novel "Crying Shadows" was published October-2013. His new novel "Midnight Oil" will be available early April-2015.

Live News
*by **Peter Hartke***

"This is Kelli Mills on location for KL5 Live! News."
Kelli Mills looked at her reflection in the mirror on the KL5 news van and studied herself critically. Her makeup was light and understated, even her lipstick was a neutral shade, her long blonde hair pulled back and done in a simple pony tail.

It gave the effect she wanted- professional, capable, strong. Her clothing fit the same motif, a black tailored skirt that came to just above the knee, a crisp white blouse that was buttoned up until right above her cleavage. Topping it off was her dark red blazer with its three silver buttons all fastened.

She stepped back so she could see more of herself and smiled. She looked good. She looked professional. She looked serious. Exactly how a reporter should. "This is Kelli Mills, reporting from the scene for KL5 Live! News."

She ran the line a few times, trying different inflections of her voice, finding which tone sounded most appropriate for the story she was about to cover. Kelli had risen to fame at KL5 as a weather girl. Her pretty face and peppy demeanor could take the sting out of even the worst storm. Her girl next door innocent persona was also very popular with men and women, and it didn't hurt that she had amazing legs and wasn't afraid to show them.

She had been at channel five for three years now, and though she loved her job, she wanted more. She didn't put all that time studying journalism in college just to tell people when it would rain. She wanted to be a serious reporter, an investigative reporter.

She had talked to Brad, the station manager, she had made an appointment and sat right in his office. She plead her case but she could tell by the glazed look on his face that he really wasn't listening. "Listen Kelli, we got a good thing going here' he said. Don't rock the boat Kel, people love you doing the weather."

"Come on Brad!" she countered, "at least let me do some of the storm remotes. I am tired of being stuck in the studio!"

"We'll see", he answered, "Let me get through this midland murderer story and we will see." he said ending the conversation.

Kelli was fuming after the meeting, she knew her face was red and she could feel the tears threaten to come. "I will not cry" she told herself as she marched down the hallway towards her dressing room. She had her head down and she was mad, mad at Brad for not listening, and mad at herself for not being more forceful.
She rounded the corner and walked right into Ronnie Steward. She gave a little frightened gasp and if Ronnie had not reached out to steady her, taking her arm, she was sure she would have fallen.

She did roll her ankle though when she slipped, her pump had landed funny and her foot bent sideways, she felt a sharp pull in her ankle then a quick flash of pain.

Ronnie still held her as she regained her footing, looking concerned as she winced a bit from the pain as she put weight on her injured ankle, he stepped closer to her, letting her support her weight against him.

"Are you OK?" he asked.

She grunted softly, nodding that she was even though she wasn't sure of it yet. She looked up at him, saw the worry in his face, and then the tears came.

"Hey.. hey.. it's alright." he said, "are you OK?, Do you think it's broken?"
Kelli just cried harder. All the anger and frustration she felt from the meeting came rushing back and overwhelmed her, drug her under like a strong riptide, and all she could do was cry.
Ronnie looked up and down the hallway for help and saw it was just him. A one man Calvary, he thought to himself, a regular fucking Dudley Do-right.

"OK... OK, Kelli. Shh, it's OK. Let's get you to your office, OK, put your arm around my shoulders. Just let me carry the weight."

Kelli nodded, still sobbing, trying, and failing to get herself under control.
She put her arm around him and they slowly hobbled to her dressing room. He reached for and opened the knob when they got there, maneuvered her across the small place and helped her sit.

He turned and grabbed the box of tissues off the desk after she was seated, pulled one out and offered it to her, "Here you go"

Kelli perched on the edge of the couch, her head down and her face in her hands, her injured ankle throbbed dully but wasn't broken as far as she could tell. She held it out in front of her, rotating her foot slowly, sucking in a quick breath of air.

Ronnie stood, watching, not sure what to do. After waiting for a few minutes, he politely cleared his throat to get her attention. "You OK then?" he asked, feeling awkward just standing there.
Kelli took a few very deep breaths, holding each on for a second before exhaling it out in a slow steady push. After a moment she got herself back under control, with just a few sobs wracking her body as she came down.

"I.. I'm so sorry Ronnie"

"Aww, hush now. Nothing to be sorry about" he said. "Do you want me to go get someone?"

She looked up at him and smiled weakly, "No, I.. I think I'm OK" She said, sitting up straighter.

"I'm really sorry to have dumped cried on you like that, Ron, you must think I'm looney. I was still upset from a meeting with Brad, that's all, our collision was just the straw that broke the camel's back."

She looked up at him sheepishly through her red, bloodshot, eyes.
"Well you should have just said so, a meeting with Brad is enough to make anyone cry!" he said laughing.

She joined him, nodding in agreement, "You know what I was feeling then." she said, smiling, "He's just not going to give in."

"Giving in on what?"

And with that simple question, she told him everything, told him of her dreams.

She hugged him before he left and thanked him for listening. He gave back a warm smile and an "any time"

He opened the door and stopped, looking back at her. "Don't let go of your dreams Kelli, you're something special, you have something people want."

She flashed him a warm smile and he gave a small wave and was gone.

"He's a nice guy" Kelli thought to herself as he left.

She didn't know Ronnie well. He was a cameraman with the station's second team, so he mostly shot the human interest stuff, not the real news. He'd only been working at the station for maybe six months and now that she saw how nice he was, she wished they had talked earlier, under better circumstances.

It was about two months later when she answered the knock on her dressing room door to find Ronnie standing there.
She had seen him around the station in that time. A lot actually. They always seemed to be crossing paths. She always said hi and greeted him with a more real smile than she bothered to give to most.

Still, she was a bit bewildered to find him at her door looking like a kid with master key to the candy shop.

"Hey Kelli, you got a min?" he asked, the excitement clear in his voice.

She really didn't. She was still getting dressed and going over the report for her next broadcast, but she could tell he was excited, and that intrigued her.

"I got a few minutes, yeah, come on in."

Ronnie glanced both ways, as if making sure the coast was clear before he walked in, closing the door behind him.

"I have to be on the air in thirty." she said, "we don't have much time before Maria will be here to do my make-up. So what's up?"

He nodded and glanced at the clock and nodded again.

"OK" he said. "I'll be fast."
He looked at her, his eyes bright, his voice low but coming fast.
"I found it Kelli. I found a story... the story.. your story. The one that's going to make those snobby news bastards have to sit up and take notice. They will have to take you seriously after this, and I'm going to ride your coattails all the way to shooting the real news!'

Kelli look at first incredulous, then interested and finally excited as what he was saying sunk in. His cat who ate the canary attitude was infectious. Yes, she thought, you don't believe I can do serious news. Well, I'm going to show you Mr. Brad Sanders!

"Tell me!" She said in a conspiratorial whisper, "Tell me what the story is!"

As if by cue, there was a knock on her door. The both turned their heads to look at it and she cursed lightly at being interrupted.

"Later," he said, "After your report. Meet me upstairs in the meeting room, it'll be empty that time of night, and I'll fill you in."

Maria knocked again and called out her name. "Kelli? You in there?"
"Yeah, one sec Mar."

"You just have to promise me one thing Kelli." he said in the same low voice. "If I get you an exclusive, you'll give me what I want too."

Kelli nodded, "Of course Ronnie, this is a big break for both of us, and I won't forget you thought of me"

"promise?"

"I promise" she said very seriously.

He smiled and took her hand and squeezed it. "See you after" he said as he opened the door and held it for Maria before leaving through it.

Kelli was giddy, she was extra perky during her segment, and even flirted back with Terry the sports guy during the crossover to the surprise and delight of the anchors.

After the show, she changed quickly, dying to know what Ronnie was onto. She hurried to the elevator, waving to the people she knew, trying to look casual. The wait for the elevator was taking forever. She kept fingering the button as if the elevator could tell she was in a hurry and would speed up to accommodate.

Finally the led display showed her floor and gave its cursory "bing" as the doors opened. She stood back and let the people off, squeezing past the last one in her impatience, and touched the number for the sixth floor.

She had the elevator to herself, most people were heading down this time of night, not going up as she was. She crossed her arms and her fingers drummed nervously on her upper arm during the short ride.

The doors opened and she stepped out, turning right and heading down the hall, past the empty offices towards the meeting room. The floor seemed deserted and dark, the only sound the soft hum of the computers, she could see the light was on in the meeting room and quickened her pace.

Ronnie saw her coming down the hall and walked to the door, opening it as she got there, and nervously peeking up and down the hall before closing it behind her.

Kelli walked into the room, tossed her bag on the large rectangular table and plopped down in one of the leather chairs, looking up at Ron. "OK, spill!" She said, finding it hard to hide her curiosity and excitement.
Ronnie smiled and nodded, "I got a scoop Kelli. A good one."

Kelli looked at him with interest and waited for him to go on, motioning with her hand for him to continue.

"Right, OK." He said, his eyes shining still with glee.

"You know how the mayor is leaning on the police to close down all of the massage parlors and pawnshops in the red light district? His whole 'let's clean up this city and make it safe for our children' campaign he's running." Ronnie imitated the radio announcer's voice when he did the tagline in the ad Mayor Davis.

Kelli nodded. It was hard to miss the ads, they had been running ad nauseam on the radio for the last month as election time drew near.

"Mayor Robert Davis. He cares about this city, and he cares about you!" Kelli said, doing her own imitation of the ad, laughing as she did.

"Yeah, that's the one" Ronnie said.

"Well, what if I told you that the squeaky clean Mayor Davis has a dirty little secret?" He said in a lower voice. "And he wasn't as clean as he lets on."

Kelli looked at him with her eyes wide, taking in what he said, whispering "Noooo!" in an excited breathless voice. If he really had the goods on the mayor, this wasn't just big, it was huge!

Ronnie smiled wider and nodded, seeing she was catching on, this was what she had been waiting for. Real news!

"I have a friend who works for some shady characters... don't ask." He said with an embarrassed tone, not proud he had such friends it seemed, then continued.
"Well, one of the guys he works for, they run this club. An exclusive club. It's a sex club but like a kinky one, ya know?"

Kelli nodded, giving rapt attention to his every word, leaning forward more as he continued.
"It's real exclusive, members have to be referred from what I hear. A lot of the city's power players visit. My friend tells me it's some sort of

bondage club, all the girls dressed in leather and carrying whips from what he says."

Ronnie saw Kelli's nose wrinkle at the mention of bondage and whips, nodding like he agreed with her. "Yes, sick huh." and she nodded in return.

"The best part.. The best part of all of this..."

He paused, meeting Kelli's wide eyes with his.

"It's in residential neighborhood, not two blocks from the elementary school, and Mayor Davis is a member!"

"No shit!' Kelli said, sounding as amazed as she felt. "No bullshit? You're sure?"

Ronnie nodded. "I'm sure. I've seen the house. From the outside anyway, but I did see the mayor go in, and my friend has no reason to lie about what goes on inside."
"Oh my god Ronnie, that's so huge! Kelli said. "That story would break this town apart!"

"Yeah" Ronnie said. "That's why I want you to be the reporter that breaks it. It's what you've been waiting for."

"What do we do?" she asked.

Ronnie went on to explain his plan. They would find out when the mayor would be there, the club was by appointment only, and his friend would know.

Then... "Then we go in rogue reporter style, cameras blazing, mics live, and catch the bastard with his pants down. Simple as that."

Kelli nodded as he talked. He was right, it was the break she had been looking for, the one that would make her a real reporter, then people would give her the respect she deserved.
She was in. Hook line and sinker in. "Just tell me when."

Ronnie said he will be in touch. She left first, he said he would be following behind so no one was suspicious of why they were together.

Kelli felt like a balloon over the next few days, like she was floating and only the thin string that was her job kept her tethered to the ground. She had been practicing in the mirror in her dressing room and her bathroom mirror at home.

She saw Ronnie here and there, and they always waved, but apparently he had no news yet. So frustrating!

It was five days after their meeting that Ronnie slipped her a note as they passed. She hurried back to her dressing room to read it, unfolding the paper, her heart racing.
"Tonight: 8 PM
Meet me at the Kennedy school.

We are going in!"

Kelli read it over and over, feeling her heart race, tonight was the night. And she was ready.

She pulled into the school parking lot at ten till eight, doing a loop around the school looking to see if Ronnie was here yet, before parking in the back of the school to wait. She readjusted her rear view mirror till she could see her lips, and practice her delivery, "This is Kelli Mills reporting live for KL5 Live!"

Kelli wrinkled her nose, that didn't sound right she thought, to many lives. She tried again, "This is Kelli Mills, on location for KL5 Live! News."

She smiled and mentally congratulated herself as she saw the KL5 Live! van drive around the corner of the school. It came around the front of her car and turned sharply, pulling in next to her, and stopping so that the vehicles were driver's side window to window.

Ronnie looked out the window of the van, gave a short wave and motioned her to roll down her window. He looked excited and nervous and she quickly opened her window.

"Hey." Ronnie started as soon as her window was open, "Grab your stuff and get in the van. Waiting on a call from my friend, then we move."

Kelli nodded, "OK", and reversed her window, took the keys out of the ignition and grabbed her bag. She stole one more quick look in the mirror and opened her door, circling around the front of the door and climbing into the passenger side.

"All set?" Ronnie said as she settled in. "Yes, I think so." She replied. "What's the plan?"
"OK, here's what's going to happen. Once I get this call, it will mean the mayor is there, then my friend going to take a break from his desk and go have a smoke out back..."
"We will get to the door, shoot a quick open, then head in. He said it's gonna look like a normal house, the action is all in the basement, so just cross the kitchen and go through the solid white door. The one with the window leads to the back porch."

"We will do a shoot at the door, then we go live, open that door, head down the stairs, mayor will be in the room with the heavy black door."

Kelli nodded, her heart thumping loudly in her chest, she worked to control her breathing. "This is the big leagues Kel, time to step up!" she told herself. Little by little she was able to calm herself down.

Ronnie got up and went to the back of the van. "Gonna do one last check of the equipment. I had to bring the small camera, the big one was being used for a remote. Seems that another girls gone missing. So, don't want anything going dodgy, we only get one shot at his," He said as he broke out his equipment.

"I can't just sit here," she said, "I have to at least stretch my legs some."

She got out of the van, checking herself in the mirror and practicing her opening. She paced a bit up and down, wanting this to happen, patience was never one of Kelli's better attributes.

Finally she heard a cell phone ring and could hear Ronnie answer. She held her breath for a moment until she heard him slide the side door of the van open and said, "We're on! Let's move."

He handed her a black oversized hoodie jacket. "Just wear it till we are inside. If anyone see's the famous Kelli Mills walking down the street it might attract too much attention."

Kelli frowned but took the jacket, pulling it on and putting the hood up gently as to not mess her hair, she hated to ruin her look but knew he was right. Ronnie gave her a microphone which she hid in one of the jacket's deep pockets.

The camera had its own case, looking kind of like an oversized briefcase, and Ronnie hefted it up, smiling at her.

"You ready to make news?" he asked her.

"You know it!" she answered returning his smile.

"You're going to do great, you got something special."

She smiled as he hefted up the case and they started walking. "Don't forget our deal when you're famous" he said grinning. "I got you a scoop."

"Don't worry." She said as they walked. "I got a good feeling. I think we will both get what we want."

Ronnie grinned at her again. "You know, I think you're right, Kelli. We play our cards right, this will be ready for the eleven o'clock"

The walk to the house took maybe five minutes, and they didn't talk much until they were only a few houses away. "OK, so you know the plan. Once we get on the porch, we do a quick opening shot. Do an intro or whatever, but be quick. The lights on the cam are bright, and we will attract attention."

She nodded, "Got it, I'm ready."

"Once we are in, I'm going to just keep shooting, so let's move quick. I don't want them to have time to realize we are there."

Kelli grabbed the mic from the jacket pocket, took off the hoodie, laying it in the grass next to the stairs. She ran her fingers through her hair, cleared her throat softly, took a deep cleansing breath and nodded to Ronnie.

"OK, I'm ready."

Ronnie had the camera out, checked it over quickly and said, "Me too, let's do it."
Kelli walked up the steps to the open porch, clearing her throat and getting in position in front of the door and giving a thumbs up to Ronnie. He put the camera on his shoulder, checked the view, and looked up at Kelli.

He started the countdown.

"Going live in 5-4-3-2-"

At one he hit the lights and started the camera recording, pointing at Kelli. She took a moment to let her eyes adjust to the bright light in her eyes, took one last deep breath, and started her report.

"Tonight, join us as we uncover a dirty little secret the mayor doesn't want you to know about. The shocking part though, It could be in your neighborhood"

Kelli paused for a moment, then drug her hand across her throat signaling for Ronnie to cut. Looking at him hopefully, she asks "Was that OK?" even though she knew it was. She felt pumped, She had nailed it!

Ronnie killed the lights on the camera. "That was perfect." He said, "Let's get inside, we gotta keep moving."
Kelli nodded, reaching and opening the door, letting him go in first with the cam, then following and closing the door softly. Kelli was struck with the seediness of the room, the carpet, a once a green sea foam, now was dark with stains and worn to its threads in places.

It was rather barren beside that, there were two small chairs set around a round dark wood table whose top was littered with burns from cigarettes and masses of rings from cups. There was an ashtray and a cup of coffee sitting on the table and the air smelled of stale smoke. The whole vibe was not what she had expected.

She had left Ronnie back by the door, and when she turned back he was locking it. He grinned at her questioning look. "Don't want anyone coming in behind us, ready to start?"

"Yes, I'm ready." She said, forgetting the vibe of the house and slipping back into the story. She cleared her throat and gave him the thumbs up. Ronnie lifted the camera and triggered on the lights. Kelli paused, counted to five in her head and started.

"Mayor Davis has run his campaign on his reputation, his stand for family values, and his war on pornography in any form."

"This reporter has discovered that apparently the mayor doesn't practice what he preaches. Tonight, this KL5 Live! reporter is going to confront the mayor on this shocking development."
Kelli turned to profile, and gestured with her hand at the room around her.

"To most, this looks like any house in any neighborhood, and in fact it is in a neighborhood. A neighborhood not two blocks away from a children's elementary school."

"In actuality this house is home to a club. A very exclusive and unusual club. A club that Mayor Davis is a member of and frequently visits."

"This club is of an adult nature and deals with the kinky side of human sexuality. Bondage, discipline, whips chains and domination are all on the menu for the club's members. Come with us now as we take you live into the heart of this residential brothel."

Kelli turned on her heels and let her face break into huge grin. She had killed it! Not a flub in the whole speech. Her mind was already at confronting the mayor, seeing the look of panic on his face, she wondered if he would be in a rubber outfit like the guy from Pulp Fiction and had to bite her lip to keep from laughing.

Ronnie followed her with the camera as she moved through the living room and through the kitchen, the lights bouncing madly along the walls as he kept shooting. She paused at the door to the basement turning to the camera. "What we are about to see may be graphic and offensive." She said before pulling the door open and stepping into the stairway.

There was a smell, more than a smell Kelli thought, a reek. It wasn't strong but enough to make her grimace when it first hit her nose. She was glad the camera hadn't been on her face for that moment!

She went down the stairs quickly now, not wanting to give anyone any time to adjust to them being here. The basement, like the upstairs gave no indication that it was anything other than a normal basement. Kelli did see the door though, exactly as described.

The smell was stronger down here, thick, and cloying. It reminded of going into her father's shed when she was a girl. In the summer, when it had "been a scorcher" as her dad always called the long hot days, going into the shed was something she dreaded.

The rancid smell of decay and the staleness of the air would about make her choke and the thickness of the air would coat her mouth for hours after, even when she tried to be quick and hold her breath while she was in there.

The basement had the same sort of smell, not as strong as the shed air, but reminiscent.
Kelli reached the bottom and turned to the camera, one hand on the doorknob, "Let's see if Mayor Davis is in, shall we?" She said, opening the door wide and letting the camera's lights spill into the room.

She started to speak again, and then turned her head and looked into the room. At first she saw what she expected to see. There was a girl on some sort of medical table in the center of the room. The table had been tilted up until the girl was almost in a standing position.

Thick straps of black leather secured her to the table at points along her arms and her legs, with longer straps attached across her midsection and shoulders, effectively pinning her to the table.

The was a red ball gag in the girl's mouth, and she was writhing on the table, the first crack in the illusion that Kelli noticed were the girl's eyes. They weren't showing pleasure or humor nor did they have that dead glassy look that was the earmark of a strung out girl.

They were wide with terror, and she screamed through her gag, saliva spraying out from the hiss sound of her voice around the ball gag and her body jerking against the bonds with all of her strength.

There was no one else in the room, where the fuck was the mayor, Kelli thought, looking around wildly before looking back at the girl. The girl was screaming in terror into her gag, but her eyes weren't on Kelli. No, her eyes were focused behind Kelli, over her shoulder.

Kelli turned, following the girl's eyes.

Ronnie had set down the camera on a crate and he was standing between it and Kelli blocking the door, the bright light from the camera showed him in a silhouette.

Kelli looked at him confused. "Ronnie, what the fuck is going on. We have to get" Her voice caught in her throat, she saw the knife in Ronnie's hand as he came closer.

"I gave you what you wanted Kelli." He said.

"I gave you a scoop, a breaking story, you got the dirt. First hand and up close. You.... you have uncovered the identity of the midland murderer."

Kelli screamed as he walked closer, raising the knife, "I gave you what you wanted Kelli, and a deal is a deal. Now give me what I want! You promised!" he screamed as he brought the knife down into her shoulder near her neck.

"I want to be covered in your blood!"

Blood spewed from where the knife entered Kelli's neck. Red, warm, thick, fresh blood. Ronnie licked some off of the blade as he held her against the doorway with his other hand.
"Mmm," he exclaimed as he tasted her blood.

"I always knew you were something special Kelli."

He brought the blade down again and again in a haze of high pitched screaming and blood.
Lots of blood.
Ronnie got what he wanted.

And with a rasping breath, Kelli Mills signed off for the last time ever.

# # #

Peter Hartke
Peter Lives in a quiet town with his wife Tiffanna and their three dogs who are more like their kids.

Happy Anniversary
by Todd Martin

Mary got out of the car and made her way to the front door, smiling down at the gift bag in her hand. Mary was not sure that whether Richard will love her gift while she couldn't wait to see the look on his face when she will present the gift to him. She couldn't help but wonder what he'd gotten her and decided that she would pretend to like it even if it wasn't exactly what she wanted. Over the years, he'd given her many gifts that she didn't really cared for but she never let him know that she didn't like them. He was a great man and a wonderful husband, but selecting the best gift for her was never one of his strong points.

As she walked up the sidewalk, she frowned when she noticed that the grass in the front yard desperately needed to be cut. It had grown higher than it ever had before and it made her worry that the neighbors would think that they were too lazy to take care of their lawn. Normally she would have marched inside and made Richard get the mower out of the garage but not today. Today was a special day. Today was their day and she didn't want to spend it arguing with him about something as pointless and silly as lawn care.

When she walked into the modest two-bedroom house they'd called home ever since they were married, Richard greeted her with a kiss and a bouquet of red roses. Since twenty years, he remembered their anniversary and always got her roses to help her celebrate the day. She never really liked roses (she thought they smelled like a funeral home) but she never let him in on this fact as she thought that it was a very sweet gesture and she didn't want to hurt his feelings.

"Happy Anniversary!" he exclaimed, giving her another kiss.

"Happy Anniversary to you too, dear!" she replied with a smile.

"Let me put these in some water for you." he said as he took the roses from her and headed towards the kitchen with them.

She carried the gift bag into the den and kicked her shoes off before sitting down on the couch. Her feet ached brutally so she sat there for a few moments rubbing them until the pain subsided. Standing on her feet all day at work was getting harder for her as she got older and she was thankful that she didn't have that many years left until she could retire. She started working at the silicone factory a week after she graduated from high school and while it paid well it was a v physically demanding job and she looked forward to the day that she would clock out for the last time.

Richard joined her in the den moments later and handed her a glass of sweet tea with a lemon in just the way she liked it. He sat down beside her and eyed the gift bag eagerly, reminding her more of a little boy than a man in his late fifties.

"Do you want to open your gift now?" she asked even though she already knew what his answer would be.

"I guess." he said, trying not to sound too excited but failing miserably.

"If you can't open it now, just wait and open it later." she said, knowing that he was dying to open it right then and there.

"Oh no, I can open it now." he said enthusiastically as he reached for his gift.

She handed him the blue gift bag with the smiling cat on the front of it and he basically snatched it out of her hand. He tore into it and threw the tissue paper over his shoulder where it landed on the back of the couch behind him. He peered down into the bag and a enormous smile crossed his lips when he saw what was inside.

"How did you know?" he asked as he pulled the set of steak knives out of the bag and admired them.

"Oh please. You've only been dropping hints about them for last three months. It wasn't very hard to figure out what you wanted!"

"I have not!" he protested with a grin on his face.

"Every time we eat you complain that the knives we have wouldn't cut butter. It was pretty obvious that you wanted a new set."

"I guess I need to work on being more subtle, huh?"

"Maybe just a little."

"Thank you very much, I love them!" he proclaimed as he took one of the knives out of the box and examined it.

"You're welcome. I'm glad you like them. I know we'll be putting them to good use soon," she said, "Speaking of which do you want me to make steak for dinner tonight?"

"I've already taken care of dinner tonight, you don't have to cook."

"What do you mean?" she asked, hoping that he hadn't tried to prepare a meal for them as he was lucky if he could boil water.

"I made reservations for us at Hoffman's at 7:00."
"You got us a table at Hoffman's? But they're so expensive!"
"It's our day sweetheart, I think we should do something special. Besides that I don't think that one meal is going to break us."

"I guess not."

"That's the spirit. Now, do you want your gift now or do you want to wait until we get back from the restaurant?"

"It'll probably be late when we get back so you better give it to me now."

"Well come on then, it's in the basement," he said as he took her by the hand and lifted her up off the couch, "I think you're really going to like what I picked out for you."

As Richard led her down the hallway they passed the spare bedroom that was used as Mary's sewing room. It was originally going to be the baby's room but after she had a miscarriage Richard had repainted it and put an old sewing machine in it for her, his way of trying to erase the past. They tried to conceive again years later with the same end result and after that Mary was afraid to attempt it again for fear that it would just result in them being heartbroken for a third time.

There were times that she regretted never having a child and even though Richard tried to pretend that he wasn't bothered by it but she knew the truth. She knew that it was her fault but he never blamed her for it, and when they would speak about it, he would always just say that for whatever reason they just weren't meant to be parents. There was a time that they considered adopting but it was going to be a long and drawn out process and Richard never quite seemed to be on board with the idea to begin with as he was uncomfortable with the idea of raising someone else's child as their own. As the years went by, both of them became content with just having cats and dogs that they considered to be their children.

They walked down the steps to the basement and Richard made her close her eyes. Not satisfied that she wasn't going to peek he got behind her and covered her eyes with his hands as he softly guided her toward the back of the basement. When he removed his hands she opened her eyes and squealed in delight when she saw her anniversary gift in front of her.

"Oh Richard, I love it!" she gushed as she gave him a quick hug.

"Good, I'm glad you're happy with it, there were several to choose from and I was worried I got the wrong one." he replied, giving her a kiss on the cheek.

Sitting in a metal armchair that Richard had made and welded to the basement floor was a very pretty young woman in her early twenties. The woman had long black hair, blue eyes and a slim and curvy body. Mary remembered her, her name was Tracy and she worked at the sporting goods store at the local mall. She had helped Mary find the perfect set of golf clubs last year for Richard's birthday. Mary knew then and there that she had to have her and when she told Richard about her she wasn't sure that he would be able to find her. She had given him a list of the women that worked at the mall that she was interested in so he would have several options, but Tracy was the one that she really had her heart set on.

Traci's hands and feet were handcuffed to the chair to make sure that she couldn't get away, and there was duct tape across her mouth to prevent her from screaming. As Mary leaned down to touch her she tried to flinch away, a look of mortal terror etched on her face. She had a black eye and her lip was swollen and caked with dried blood, suggesting that she had put up a lot of resistance when Richard had gotten her. She tried to say something but couldn't make it due to the fact that her mouth was taped shut. So, she just grinned and nodded at her politely.

"She's perfect! Even better than the one that you got last year!" Mary exclaimed, feeling as if she might burst into tears of happiness.
"I wasn't sure which one to get, there were several on your list that I followed around before I decided on this one." he replied as he motioned at Traci.

"I'm glad you picked her, she was the one that I wanted the most. You did a great job! Thank you!"

"You're very welcome. Just be careful, she's a feisty one. I almost never got her in the car, she put up a hell of a fight in the car just like…"

"Just like Cheryl did all those years ago." Mary finished for him.

"Exactly. Can you believe that today is the twentieth anniversary of the day we killed Cheryl? Where does the time go?"

"I know, it seems like it was just yesterday."

"Go ahead," Richard said as he took the digital camera out of his pocket, "take some pictures of her for the album."

Mary took the camera from him and walked in front of Traci with it. She snapped a couple of pictures of her from the front and then walked around her in a circle making sure to get shots of her from all angles. When she was done she reviewed the pictures with Richard and was satisfied with how they turned out. There was one from the front that she was particularly pleased with as it really showed the terror in Traci's eyes. Richard on the other hand was fond of one of the pictures taken from the side as it captured her in the process of struggling with one of the handcuffs as she tried to free herself.

"Go ahead and get in there beside her, I'll get a few of you together." Richard instructed as he took the camera back.

"Can I take the tape off her mouth?" Mary asked as she walked back over to Traci. "If I remember correctly she has such nice teeth and it would make a better picture if she was showing them off."

"Nah, we better not, I don't want her screaming and yelling, somebody might hear her."

Mary shrugged in disappointment and draped her arm over Traci's shoulder. She didn't really think that anyone would hear her if they removed the tape but she decided not to make an issue out of it. She posed in a variety of positions with Traci as Richard snapped a handful of shots. He took several with Mary leaning beside her, one with her standing behind her with her hands on Traci's shoulders, and one with her reaching over to give her a kiss on the cheek.

"Beautiful, just beautiful," Richard said as he reviewed the pictures, "these are going to look great in the picture album."

"Do you want to see the little album we've put together?" Mary asked as she ran her fingers through Traci's hair lovingly, "We've got photos of every single girl we've killed in the last twenty years in there."

"I'll have to go get it, it's upstairs." Richard said.

"Then go get it, I think she'll like looking at it," Mary replied, "Grab your new knives while you're up there too so we can get to work."

"Right, I'm eager to see if those babies are as good as they claim." he said as he made his way up the steps.
When Mary heard the footsteps overhead and knew for certain that he was upstairs she turned to Traci and took the tape off of her mouth. She attempted to scream almost immediately as Richard had predicted but Mary put her hand over her mouth to stop her.
"Now let's have none of that, no one will hear you anyway and you'll only end up making him angry." Mary said in a soft voice, "Trust me, you don't want to do that."

She took her hand away a few seconds later when she felt confident that she wasn't going to scream at the top of her lungs. Traci's lip quivered in fear and Mary couldn't help but notice how beautiful she was even in her current state. Tears started to stream down her cheeks and Mary found it to be so endearing that it made her want to give her a hug and ensure her that everything was going to be fine. She felt a strange connection to Tracy more than she had with any of the other girls and for a moment she actually considered letting her go until she realized what would happen to her and Richard if she did.

"Please…please let me go." Traci whispered in a choked voice.

"You know I can't do that honey." Mary answered.

"I won't tell anyone, I swear!"

"You say that now but you'd change your mind later."

"I swear to God I won't tell a single soul!"

"I wish I could believe you but I just can't."

"Why? Why are you doing this to me?" Traci sobbed.

Before Mary could give her an answer she heard Richard coming back down the steps and quickly put the tape back over her mouth. She wiped the tears away from Traci's cheek and gave her a kiss on the forehead as he approached them with the picture album in one hand and the steak knife set in the other.
"Here you go." he said as he handed her the album and then started taking the knives out of the box.

Mary sat down on the floor beside Traci and started showing her the pictures that were in the album. The first half of the album, which Mary told her was the "Before" section showed pictures of countless women bound to the very chair that Traci was currently occupying. Traci noticed that Mary was in every picture as well, posing and smiling for the camera as she stood beside each frightened-looking woman as she had done earlier with her. It was obvious from the style of dress that the women were wearing and the quality of the photos that this had been their little hobby for many years and she couldn't help but wonder how they hadn't gotten caught by now.

Mary thumbed through the album to what she referred to as the "After" section and what Traci saw almost made her sick. There were pictures of all the same women after they had been murdered in the most brutal ways imaginable. There was one in particular that had a woman around her age with a screwdriver imbedded in her eye socket that really disturbed Traci, and to her horror as Mary continued to turn the pages the pictures only got worse.

"See this one? We used hedge clippers on her," Mary said proudly as she pointed to the picture of a decapitated woman, "I believe it was back around 1988 or '89."

"I remember that! That was a fun one!" Richard contributed as he laid the knives out on a workbench.

"Oh this one brings back memories!" Mary exclaimed gleefully as she pointed at one of the pictures, "Richard thought it would be a good idea to use a chainsaw on her. What a mess! There was blood and body parts everywhere! It took me forever to clean up afterward!"

"I helped you clean!" he replied in a gruff voice from over his shoulder. Mary showed her a few more pictures, explaining in great detail what was used on each woman before she shut the album and smiled down at Traci.

"Richard didn't tell you about our tradition did he?" she asked as she rubbed Traci's shoulders, "Every year on this day he gets me a special gift like you and I give him some sort of tool or weapon."

"Then we use whatever tool she got me on the gift I got her," he added as he picked up two of the largest knives and looked at them, "I think that if more couples spent such quality time together then there would be a lot fewer divorces in the world, don't you think?"

"Just be glad you weren't here the year that I got him a sledgehammer," Mary said with a chuckle, "I'm sure you could tell by the picture I showed you just how painful that had to be."

"Look on the bright side, at least we're just going to use knives this year," Richard said as he approached them with the knives in his hands, "Sure, it's going to hurt but it won't be as bad as having your face smashed in with a sledgehammer or having your limbs cut off with a chainsaw."

"This is the twentieth anniversary of our first kill and I guess we were feeling a little nostalgic," Mary informed her, "We just used knives on Cheryl that day and wanted to honor her by using them on you too. She was such a lovely girl. If it makes you feel any better I think that you're a lot prettier than she was though."
"She won't be prettier for much longer, these knives are fantastic!" Richard said as he handed her one of the knives.
"I take it that you're happy with your gift then?" she asked
"Very much. Are you pleased with yours?"
"Of course I am!"

"Shall we then?" he asked as he raised the knife above Traci's head.

"We shall." she replied, doing the same with her knife.

"Happy anniversary, Mary."

"Happy anniversary to you too, may we have many, many more." she said before they brought the knives down in unison on Traci's head.

# # #

Todd Martin
Todd Martin grew up in Irvington, a small town in Kentucky. Thanks to his mother, father, and favorite uncle he started watching horror films at a very young age and has been a horror geek ever since. His first book, Nightmare Tales was published in 2006 and he has had several short stories published in a number of horror collections as well as on Creepypasta.com since then. His short script Lucky was one of the winners of the Unscripted 3 screenwriting contest and the film was voted the overall winner of the film festival itself. He currently writes articles, conducts interviews, and reviews movies and books for Horrornews.net

A Civil War Story

*by **Wally Holderness***

"Sergeant, we were told to go out, capture members of Mosby's Rangers, bring back the partisans to Captain Cole at Warrenton, and that's that. You order me to charge into a small farmhouse. You start shooting, killing two women and three kids; any of Mosby's men around? No. Burning the farmhouse to the ground won't hide what we did here."

"Shut up, Private Bixby! Maybe you forgot who's in charge!"

"You're in charge; I'm just worried," says the thin but muscularly built twenty year-old private, born and raised on a small Vermont farm. Though he is slight of build, he is of a violent temper, ready to use his fists to settle problems. "Here we are in the Virginia backcountry, who knows where," says Bixby.

"Private, we are just outside of Rector's Cross Roads near Goose Creek, ok?"

"Yeah, Sarge, in the middle of Mosby's Confederacy." With fear in his voice, the private says,

"They'll kill us you know."

"Listen and listen good," says Sergeant Hennessy, a wicked character ten years Bixby's senior. A burly man with a full beard, Hennessy thinks the Civil War is a time for a killer like him to commit his evil acts. "I charged into that place thinking there were Rangers holed up in there. Mistakes happen; this was a mistake. I'll get us out of this fix." It is a dark December night in Northern Virginia, 1863. The largest snowstorm in years is pounding down on the two murders. Private Bixby had charged into the small two-room farmhouse behind the sergeant, leaving when Hennessy started to shoot, deciding to stand outside with the mounts, and waiting for Sergeant Hennessy to complete his murderous deed. He was a willing accomplice to the killings, helping burn down the farmhouse in which the two families had been waiting out the cold snowy night. Their husbands, members

"

of Mosby's Rangers, were out capturing a Union wagon train near Aldie, Virginia. The rage of Mosby and his Rangers would befall these two Union cavalrymen, once their deed was discovered. So it was that very night, by six Rangers not on a raid, but given the task of checking the well-being of families in the area. Once the Rangers rode up to the smoking ruins of the Taylor farm containing the snow-covered charred remains of two families, Private Bixby and Sergeant Hennessy became game to be hunted down and hanged from the nearest tree. With the prints of men and horses still fresh in the snow, the rangers knew the killers didn't have much of a lead.

"We walk our horses out, head to the Ashby Gap Turnpike, mount, and head east. Now let's get out of here before we do get seen by Mosby."

"Great idea, Sergeant. One problem —we can't see three feet in front of us. The snow is up to our knees, and guess what else—we are going' to freeze out here."

"Just follow me, Private, and keep your mouth shut." No sooner does the sergeant speak these words than the sound of muffled rifle shots in the distance is heard by the two cavalrymen-turned-desperados. "Private Bixby, did you see where those shots came from?"

"No, I can't see a thing, Sergeant."

"Well, forget about it; just mount and we'll try to put some distance between us, that farm, and those rebs." The two cavalrymen mount their horses and head eastward through a thicket of pine trees. As they guide their horses deeper into the snow-covered woods, the Sergeant, leading the way, doesn't notice that they have approached Goose Creek's icy river embankment. The sergeant's horse tumbles into the freezing creek, head first, immediately killing it and causing the sergeant to be thrown into the creek, breaking his left arm in the fall. The rifle fire has become more rapid and greater in magnitude. Mosby's Rangers are rapidly closing the distance. "Private, you ain't going to be leaving me behind!"

"Don't worry sergeant! I think if I can get you on my horse, then we can move on."

"Yeah, get me on your horse fast!" The private is more fearful with the nearness of the rifle fire, feeling some anguish now for his actions of that night. Private Bixby dismounts his skittish horse and helps the struggling Sergeant up. The gunfire they have been hearing is now the sound of handguns. The six determined Rangers are closing in, and Private Bixby and Sergeant Hennessy can hear and see the bullets flying around them, snow being thrown up with the impact of rifle and handgun fire, brittle branches falling from trees. "Fire back at them, Private! What are you waiting for?"

"Sergeant, I can't shoot without my rifle; throw it to me Quick!" Just as he says that, Bixby's horse rears its front legs and gallops away, throwing dirty snow and ice up into the cold air, the sergeant bounding away with the private's Spencer rifle secured to the saddle. Bixby had tripped and fallen into the partially frozen creek when the horse leaped. Now, soaking wet, he jumps up from the cold water to hear Sergeant Hennessy shout out, "You're on your own, Private! One of us has to make it back!" Bixby is left to fend for himself with only his army colt revolver in his holster; the revolver being wet would never fire. If it could fire he would have killed that scoundrel sergeant, himself. With no time to think and bullets hitting tree trunks and ricocheting off rocks, he could think only of running as fast as he could in the ankle deep creek. As he starts to run he takes a quick look back and sees all six rangers. Four he can see galloping away in the direction of Sergeant Hennessy. He quickly thinks of Hennessy, hoping those Confederates catch him and hang him from the tallest tree.

He comes to his senses realizing two of the Rangers are firing at him. As he turns to run, he feels a sharp pain in the back of his left shoulder, throwing him, again, face first into the creek. Even with the darkness and the incessant snowfall, he can see, as he lay in the creek, large amounts of his bright red blood flowing downstream. The agonizing pain he has been feeling fades away fairly fast; Bixby thinking the intense cold may have numbed the pain. He turns his head expecting those two rangers to be riding up to him, revolvers drawn. But they are nowhere to be found. Private Bixby is now alone feeling bewildered but relieved by the sudden disappearance of the rebels. They had been closing in on him as they fired in his direction, so where did they go? Bixby slowly rises up from the stream, an icy cold wind swirling around him, causing a light mist of snow to brush against his face. He believes he passed out from the gunshot wound and the rebels, leaving him for dead, then took off into the dense forest, seeking their friends in the hunt for Hennessy. As he looks around, he sees a beacon of light deep in the woods, probably a farm maybe a mile away. Knowing he is in partisan country, he fears approaching an enemy dwelling. His hope is that this will be a friendly haven; otherwise, it is sure death in these woods. Heading in the direction of the distant light, the numbness he is experiencing makes his walk through the deep snow unbearably hard, the night being so much darker without the help of a glowing moon.

He approaches the beam of light, and to his amazement, discovers a gigantic Gothic mansion. He reaches a large porch, climbs three steps, walks slowly to the large front door, and knocks several times. Then taking a step back, he admires the Gothic styling of the mansion. Having been in this part of Fauquier County with fellow troopers on raids looking for Mosby, he never noticed such a sprawling mansion. He staggers back when the giant door swings open; Bixby cocks his head to get a quick glance at who's answering, ready to draw his still wet revolver from his holster. If the person answering the door shows any signs of hostility, fear of possibly being shot may make the occupant think twice about any violence. The thought of killing again is the last thing Bixby wants.

"Hello there, young man. Lost soldier, I take it?" Bixby feels overwhelming relief upon seeing an old man probably in his eighties, thin as a rail, wearing a black frock coat that shows signs of extreme wear and tear, pantaloons that don't quite reach his ankles, with torn brogans covering his feet. It looks like he can barely stand, let alone put up a fight.

Bixby replies to the old man's inquiry, "I'm just trying to get back to my unit in Warrenton before daybreak."

"You, young man, are a long ways from Warrenton. Pray tell, you all have a mighty long trek in a storm that's never endin.' By the looks of that wound— well, I don't see it happening'. Anyways come in out of the cold. Don't want you a thinkin' I'm a bad host," says the old man.

"Thank you very kindly," Bixby responds. The thought running through Bixby's mind is gratitude, being able to walk into a warm shelter and still being alive.

"What's your name, boy? The folks around these parts call me Enki, Master Enki to be precise."

"Bixby is my name. What are you? A slave owner?"

"No, no," laughs the old man, with a shrill, unnerving laugh. "Most folks who enter my dominion are entering of their own free will, just like you. Many soldiers, lately, and I welcome them fellas," says Enki with a big grin.

Bixby takes his first real look around and asks, "You don't really have much furniture in this big mansion, and why are all the windows boarded?"

"You're right," says the old man with a grin; this is kinda like a reception area to my domain."

"What are you talking about, old man? What domain?" With that, hundreds of repugnant black bats start flying all over the room; the smell is like burning flesh. Bixby dives to the floor to keep from getting hit by these disgusting beasts. "What's going on here, old man?" Bixby jumps up, swatting at bats with his revolver and shouting, "Get out of my way, whoever you are!"

"Where do you think you a goin', boy? If you are thinkin' of leavin', think twice," says Enki. "Are you thinking' you just happened to find this place? Wrong. You are so wrong! You were summoned here!" shouts old man Enki. Bixby drops his revolver and runs to the door, the bats making his retreat difficult. The door won't open, no matter how hard he tries. Bixby closes his eyes and puts his hands over his ears, trying to avoid the abhorrent sounding bats and fearful of opening his eyes, not wanting to see the old man. "Do you really think you survived that gunshot? It went through your heart, and you died a painful death in that creek!" Enki shouts, and then laughs a blood-curdling laugh. "Do you want to know what happened to your Sergeant Hennessy? You got your wish! Open your eyes and look!" Bixby tries to keep his eyes closed but here's a painfully loud wailing sound. It's Hennessy screaming. Bixby opens his eyes to see Hennessy hanging upside down on a very tall cross in total flames, his arms flailing away in the air.

Enki laughingly shouts, "Your sergeant is finally where he belongs, don't you think?" Bixby then looks directly at the old man who is changing before his eyes. His features are changing, no longer an old man, but a repugnantly sinister creature rising up as high as the twelve foot arched ceiling, large horns protruding from a misshapen head, with eyes that are large, yellow, and piercing, Bixby screams in complete fear and disgust when the monster's serpent like black tongue protrudes, from a mouth with snake-like lips. Gigantic wings expand from a scaly body that starts to glimmer with what appear as bright shining diamonds. "Welcome to hell!" shouts Satan in gleeful laughter.

Bixby looks around with deep anguish and dread, watches immense flames lapping around him, hears horrible screaming and wailing coming from condemned souls of hell. Bixby, himself, begins screaming in horror, pain, and eternal remorse.

# # #

Wally Holderness

As a child growing up in Illinois, I loved history particularly the American Civil War. When taking a break from history books, enjoyed the occasional horror story. My career took me to Washington D.C, where in my free time I became a Civil War re-enactor. Living in Virginia and Maryland each steeped in history, I spent many hours re-living battles that were fought long ago. Some battlefields give an eerie sensation that those who fought and died there, came back to again re-live the battle they fought and died on.

The Man And The Little Boy
*by **Ruhaani***

This man was working with Himachal forest department, and his job required frequent transfers to new places. During one of such transfers, he was sent to a remote village near Chamba. This place is breathtakingly beautiful and is thickly forested. He got accommodation in two storied apartment quite near to his office.

Few days passed and he had just begun to like this new place. One night this man had a dream, in his dream, he saw a little stranger, a boy of age around five years lying next to him in his bed and he is holding a handball. This boy asked the man whether he would like to play with him. The man agrees and took this small boy to the rooftop and starts playing with him. After some time, he hears a scream of that boy and that boy vanishes in the dream. Suddenly the man anxiously got up from his dream. He looked around as if the kid was there with him, but felt relaxed after he found nothing and thought it was just a dream.

Next morning when he was rushing to his office, the person who is staying on the second-floor asked him, what he was doing on the rooftop at midnight. The man got a shock after listening to this and got a little frightened, though he didn't say anything to that man and rushed quickly from there. The whole day he was contemplating as what would have happened. Finally, he convinced himself to relieve himself from this anxiety that he must have walked in his dream or maybe that second-floor neighbor is playing a prank on him.

This night even though a lot of thoughts were going inside his mind but he was trying to stay calm and let go that dream. Finally, he was able to sleep. But again he saw a dream. And he saw that boy again; standing and crying near his room and the boy starts coming closer and closer to him, and the man sees that the boy is bleeding as well. The kid was looking dreadful. He suddenly got up from his dream and felt some noise outside his room towards the main door. He switched on the lights, put on his glasses, looked all around but found nothing. He thought that it was just his imagination as he kept on thinking of that dream and that boy the whole day. But somewhere he had some doubts in his mind, and he was giving some assurances to soothe himself.

Now the next night he didn't get the dream of that boy and could sleep profoundly. He got a respite that those dreams were nothing but bad and silly nightmares only. He passed his whole day peacefully in his new office with new responsibilities and meeting new people. He came late in the evening after having a party with his Department people. He was exhausted and quickly went to sleep, without imagining that this is going to be the worst night of his entire life. That boy again came into his dream, and he sees that the boy is sitting on his belly and kept his handball on his (man's) chest. Boy's eyes and forehead are bleeding badly. The man couldn't breathe, and he woke up scared. The moment he opened his eyes, he got thunderstruck to see the boy sitting on him and he could touch boy's hair and body. Not only this, there was blood on his bed. The man's whole body started trembling` and he tried to run but he was unable to do so as this boy became much heavier than he looked. And the boy did nothing but kept asking him to play the ball with him. He tried his best to get rid of that boy from him, but couldn't do so. So he offered to play ball with him at their rooftop. And he asked the boy to let him get up, and once the boy got up, he immediately ran out of his room and kept on running away from the house as fast as he could. The man felt as if he was hearing the sound of bouncing ball following him for a long time even after he got out of his house. He didn't stop until he reached one of his colleague's house where he had a party with him. His friend took him to his place, and he stayed there for the night.

This time, the man was sure that this is not just a nightmare, but there is something wrong with the house. Next day he decided to leave that place but before that he decided to uncover the matter. He started finding out with the neighbors and the families residing near his place, and then finally he got to know that there used to live a happy couple few years back. They gave a birth to a baby boy after a very long time. They were living a happy life. The person was an air force pilot and suddenly one day he died in some plane crash. At that time his son was five years old only. So his wife started working to run his home. She kept a maid to take care of his home. This maid was very tricky and many times used to steal things from the house. One day this maid along with her husband made a plan to run away with all the money and precious possessions in the house. While they were stealing all the stuff, the boy who was playing out came inside his mother's room and saw both of them with cash and jewelry. To scare him they thrashed him severely, and he started bleeding. The boy started crying and screaming, so they tied his hands, legs with a rope, and his mouth with a sticky tape and kept the boy in the storeroom and closed it from outside. They stole all the stuff and ran away. The little boy was in extreme pain and couldn't help himself, and after struggling for some time he died there only. The Boy's mother was not able to cope up with this incident and became insane, and finally, she also left that place and went to stay with her mother's.

After this incident, two families did come to stay in this house, but they too found something wrong in there and left it immediately.Even few people claimed to have spotted that boy playing with his ball on the rooftop or outside that house in midnight with blood on his body and many times strange screams of that same boy are still heard and felt by people staying nearby.

# # #

Ruhaani

Ruhaani is young, talented and passionate storyteller in horror and fiction genre. She has incredible piece of short stories in her collection, which are published across various platforms.
She loves to travel across the globe and meet people from different cultures and background. Besides her incredible piece of short stories, she is a Badminton player and a passionate cook who tries to experiment with different spices, flavours and creating dishes from scratch.

There's Something In My Closet
*by **Luke Mepham***

Adam was slowly finishing off his evening coffee when Sophie, his daughter, called down to him.
"Daddy, when is Mommy coming home?"
"Not long now, she said she wouldn't be late"

He waited what seemed to be an eternity for the reply to come.

"Okay."

He went back to watch the rest of his TV show.

After an hour or so, Sophie came downstairs in her pajamas. "Can you read me a story?
Mummy is taking too long."

He lowered his glasses and looked over at her innocent big brown eyes. 'How could I say no?' he thought.

"Sure"

He got up and carried her upstairs and into her bed. He sat at the end of the bed amongst Mr. Fluffy the cuddly gorilla and Daisy the cuddly sheep. Everything had a name and ended with 'the cuddly' and then the name of the animal it was meant to be.

"Comfy?" she asked him then giggled
"Very, which story do you want?"
"Make one up. I want a new story"

"Okay"
He thought for a while and then made a funny story up involving the stuffed toys in her bed. He did all different kinds of voices and noises for them. She laughed and giggled and had a riot but eventually she fell into the land of nod after exhausting herself out.

He tucked her in and kissed her forehead then went to her light and turned it off before leaving. 'Did the wardrobe just open?' he thought.

He looked again and then shrugged it off as nothing. The door was always crooked.

An hour later, after he himself had dozed off, Sophie called from her bedroom.

Startled and nearly spilling his small whiskey on him he snapped himself together and called up to her.

"What's wrong?"

"Daddy, come here."

He walked upstairs holding a towel in case she has to bath after wetting the bed. He got to the door and peered inside.

"What is it, honey?"

Her face was sad. He's seen almost every expression from her but this one was new.

"Daddy, I'm scared."
"Why?"
"The wardrobe monster"

His eyes shifted on to the wardrobe and it was how he last saw it.

"Sophie, there's no such things as monsters. Do you remember that discussion we had when it was all in your imagination?"

She slowly nodded then tucked herself back down.

"Goodnight, sweetie"
It was around midnight when he was summoned again.
"Daddy"

Again he was startled and this time nearly urinated on the floor as he was taking his midnight piss session as he calls it.

He zips up and goes to her room.

She's sitting up by her pillows now and looks really pale.

"Honey, you're really going to have to try to get some sleep, it's a school night."

She looked at him, quite surprised.

"Daddy, look."

She pointed at the wardrobe and when he looked over at it, he got a strange shudder run down his back. The wardrobe door is shut.

"What is it, Sophie?"
"I caught the monster."

She smiled with happiness.

"You caught the monster…what monster?"

"The one I told you about. Go and see if you don't believe me."

Not to be outsmarted by his five year old, Adam Portlo walked to the wardrobe and opened it then turned to Sophie.

"See there's nothing in here "

"Daddy"

He'd heard that voice before. He turned around and looked down to see Sophie crouched down at the bottom of the wardrobe. She's holding her legs and her face is wet from crying. "Daddy, there's something in my bed."

# # #

Luke Mepham

Luke Mepham is a writer born and raised in the West Sussex area of England. His interest in horror started when he was 6 after he watched Dawn Of The Dead late one night. Since then he was hooked. These days he is heavily influenced by anything horror and The Twilight

Zone and in the stories he writes, he enjoys to "pull the rug from beneath the readers". He has several short film scripts that have been made into films and feature length scripts that has caught the attention of filmmakers in Hollywood.

"I'm not easily scared but I do enjoy giving other people nightmares".

The (dis)appearance
by Vardan Partamyan

And I open the door and I step inside. I am in my apartment. It is mid afternoon and the still warm autumn sun fills my home with a warm glow. I just returned from… I try to recall where exactly I returned from but get only disjointed images - people walking in the street; a window through which I can see a couple sitting and drinking coffee and laughing; a child that smiles at me from his throne on his father's shoulders; a sports car speeds past me reflecting the world in its bright red body; a woman in a grey dress is walking away - somehow I know she wants to look back but will not. All of these random images somehow come together and collide in my head and I have to close my eyes to regain the sense of reality.

It is her day off and she should be home. I call her name but there is no answer. I start walking through the apartment. Some of the windows are open and the wind is gently playing with the curtains. There is sense of peace that should be there but is not. I try to understand what is wrong and only then notice the strange silence. In a big city you never really hear nothing (unless you're dead). There is always one especially annoyed driver who wants to share his dissatisfaction with the world by honking away what could only be a string of profanities. There is always a neighbor who turns his TV up just a little bit too much and you are suddenly aware of the fact that one of the characters in his favorite soap opera has fallen into a coma after finding out that he was the father of his future wife. There is always the sound of music coming from nowhere and everywhere. There is always the not so gentle hum of the mega polis – the breathing of a giant beast. But now there was nothing.

I go into the kitchen expecting to see her cooking dinner but only emptiness stares back at me. A bit worried now, I call her name again. My voice rings strange in the great silence. I go through the apartment again and after making sure that she was not home, decide to call her. I take out my cell phone and search for her name in my address book. I search again and again, thinking that I have made a mistake but still cannot find her name. I must have deleted it by mistake when I was (a child that smiles at me from his throne on his father's shoulders)… out. As I go through my phone again and again, something strange catches the corner of my eye. I am in the corridor with our family photos hanging on the both sides. I remember us choosing them together. The photo that has caught my attention is a group photo from one of the New Year parties. I remember us there together and I remember the photograph but for some reason she was not in the picture. Must be my nerves playing pranks on me. I move on to the next picture with us on the beach, at least I was sure that we were both in the picture but in this one I was standing alone. The next picture was taken in Mauritius during our honeymoon (I remember we were so drunk that the shot had come out like a Dali picture). The Dali effect was still there but she was not. I went through all the photos, one by one but she had disappeared from all of them.

As the initial shock of my discovery recedes a bit, the ever efficient rationalizations start to kick in - this must be some kind of a mistake or, which is more likely, a very bad joke. Today's technology can do miracles far more impressive than removing a person from a photograph. The same goes for deleting her number from my address book - she could have done it while I was in the shower. I try to remember if it is our wedding anniversary or some other memorable date which could provoke this kind of a prank. We have been married for … (and my memory plays another speeding car/smiling child trick on me) … several years now and we did get married in autumn and I am sure that it was on September 16. And whatever today's date is (a woman in a grey dress is walking away - somehow I know she wants to look back but will not)... one thing is for sure – I have no idea. This is useless and I feel that just standing in the corridor will, literally, get me nowhere.

I go to our bedroom and open a random closet. Somehow, I know what I am seeing but my eyes refuse the register the emptiness that is looking back at me. I open the next closest – the same emptiness is waiting for me there. In the next one, I find my own clothes – it seems like everything is just as I have left it in the morning (which morning?). I take a deep breath and try to push away the rage that is slowly but surely rising inside me (she left you, buddy, deal with it!). Carefully controlling my pace, I head into the bathroom. My razor, brush and shampoo are in the usual places - all her things are simply gone (she is gone, old friend!). I can no longer control my anger. I run back to the bedroom kicking all the closets open (expecting to find her there? She is with someone else right now!). I run to the living room, to the study, to the balcony, through the corridor with the incomplete photographs, through the guest rooms and appear back in the kitchen. Everywhere I go I try to find a little trace of her but there is none. I take out my phone and once again look for her name – it is simply not there. I smash my phone on the wall and watch with a sort of perverted satisfaction at how it cracks open spilling its electronic guts. This sends me on a kind of destruction rampage. I kick the TV and send electric sparks flying joyfully through the air, I smash the cabinets and dishes, appliances and furniture, I throw chairs at the once priceless souvenirs and artifacts we had brought back from our (our or your?) various trips, I watch them break and feel how my own life is falling apart with them.

I don't know how long this rampage lasts but it leaves me utterly exhausted. The anger is gone together with much of my strength and will to move on. Nevertheless I keep walking around our (or is it just mine now?) apartment, quietly calling out her name as if thinking that I might have scared her and trying to convince her that there is nothing to worry about, that her husband (are you sure you are married at all?) is not mad at her.

The answer was silence and emptiness. As I kept walking around the house, all I could hear was my own footsteps and the sound of my broken heart beating in my chest.
I am not sure how long I have been walking around my apartment in my odyssey of despair. There is no watch on my hand although I usually don't take it off. It must have fallen victim to my fury just like almost every valuable item in my home. The sun isn't helping either as it still filling the house with the same warm and welcoming light as when I just came back home, what feels like an eternity ago.

The self evident conclusion finally dawns upon me – she is gone…even more, maybe she was never here to start with. My memories of our life together were just a product of my imagination, which was always a bit too vivid for my own good. There is no point in walking around the house anymore. My head feels like a thousand nuclear warheads have just detonated inside it. I am not sure about anything anymore.

It is just amazing how our imagination can build these complex structures out of our wishes, desires and aspirations. You then enter these structures and start living inside looking at the world out of the window of your castle in the sky. It feels safe inside – a bit too safe to ever want to step outside. How much of my life have I spent inside this castle? I am not sure. And again I try to recall where I was today (a woman in a grey dress is walking away - somehow I know she wants to look back but will not) but just cannot concentrate enough to actually remember anything but disjointed images I must have made up myself. My thoughts are a confused waste pieces of reality mixed with twisted products of my ever productive imagination.

I finally sit down on the floor and blankly stare at the wall in front of me with eyes that no longer want to see. The wall is covered with strange shadows and my industrious brain starts to transform the shapes I see into various figures and recollections – more castles in the sky. Here we are walking on the streets of an old town, here we are on the beach together, here is the huge antique wardrobe that took up much of our old apartment, here is the first rose I gave to her, here is… There seems to be a blurred spot on the wall that is not a shadow or a creation of my imagination. I disregard it and continue my shadow hunting. Here is the bridge that I crossed every day going to school in the town I grew up in, here is the tattoo I always wanted to get but never got it done…but the blurry shape is still there and my eyes keep shifting to it.

I get up, reluctantly, my head is heavy and my limbs no longer want to accept orders from the madman who strained them so mercilessly. I approach the wall nevertheless and try to erase the spot with the sleeve of my shirt. It seems like something is written there. I rub harder and harder trying to uncover the letters which I am now sure are there – just beyond the surface. I can see an A and a U. I take off my shirt and continue to rub with a feverish determination. Nothing else seems to matter anymore and I am somehow sure that whatever is written there is very important. Slowly, one by one, the letters start to surface. An indefinite time later, I step back. I am breathing heavily. Sweat is trickling down my forehead and into my eyes. I make an effort to clear my sight and finally I can read the writing on the wall. Finally the disjointed letters come together. I immediately recognize her handwriting. The hidden message spells two simple words – wake up.

…a woman in a grey dress is walking away - somehow I know she wants to look back – she does and it is her… I wake up.

\# \# \#

Vardan Partamyan

Vardan Partamyan was born in Yerevan, Armenia, in 1983. After returning from studies in the US, he enrolled in the Yerevan State University - majoring in Political Science and English language. In the years that followed, he was an author of and contributor to a number of non-fiction publications mainly dealing with the issues and challenges facing his newly independent country. Writing fiction has been a long time passion/obsession for Vardan who mixes influences from writers such as Stephen King, J.R.R. Tolkien, Harry Harrison, Alfred Bester, Ernest Hemingway and Ian Fleming with the eternal themes of a man's strive for freedom, the quest for self discovery and the knowledge of the unknown, presented on the backdrop of sometimes fantastical surroundings and events.

Captive
*by **Peter Hartke***

She awoke slowly, her head pounding. She opened her eyes for a moment but the brightness of the light made her close them again in pain. She felt each beat of her heart throb softly in her brain and moaned softly. She tried to raise her hand to shield the light from her eyes and it was then she realized her hands were restrained.

Her eyes shot open and she tried to lift her head to see her hands. Crashing white pain ripped through her skull and it felt as if it would split her head wide open. She laid there for a few moments, fighting not to pass out as the pain echoed through her brain. She concentrated on slowing her breathing, and little by little, the pain faded.

She opened her eyes again, a bit at a time, ready to slam them shut at the first hint of pain. The room was not as brightly lit as she first thought. Two low wattage light bulbs shone from bare fixtures mounted on an unfinished, cobweb covered ceiling. They cast twin pools of dirty yellow light pooling just past her head and her feet.

She turned her head slowly to the left inviting another small wave of pain to flash through her head. Her eyes were drawn first to the light streaming in from a small window near the top of the rough cinder block wall. It was wide but short and had a small crank attached to open it.

She let her eyes run down and along the wall and saw it was dominated by a large crude workbench. It was made from unfinished two by fours and pieces of pegboard nailed sloppily together. She could see old, rusted tools and scraps of wood and wire scattered along its top, covered in a thick layer of dust.

It took a few minutes for her to turn her head from the left over to the right. Brief flashes of pain accompanied each movement making her feel slightly nauseous. She closed her eyes for a moment to fight down the feeling. She opened them slowly and as her focus sharpened she saw a set of basic, open stairs running up along the right side of the wall.

They were old, the wood unpainted, dirty, and splintered in places. Thick cobwebs ran in between most of the treads and along the crude railing. Her eyes ran up each stair and she could see the bottom of a door at the top and a thin band of light between it and the floor.

Under the stairs there were scattered items piled along the wall. Old musty looking boxes, some ripped and spilling their contents along the floor. They were stacked one on top of the other in tilting piles. It looked like mostly old newspapers and magazines from what she could see. Nothing that would provide any immediate help with her situation.

Her head seemed to be clearing a bit, so she risked again raising it and looking down at her left hand. There was a cheap looking vinyl and Velcro hand cuff encircling her wrist, the kind one would get at a novelty shop or an adult store, a toy, not a serious restraint.

A small chain was attached to the D-ring on the cuff and ran to a small eye bolt secured into the wood table table she was laying on. Pulling her right hand up, she could tell without looking it was bound similarly.

She forced herself to breath slow, feeling the panic wanting to rise in her like a wildfire. She tried to remember what had happened, how she had gotten here, wherever here was. Her brain felt sluggish and slow, not wanting to work correctly, and struggled to recall the information she wanted.

She heard footsteps above her and her body froze. It had been quiet till then and the footfalls sounded very loud after the silence. They echoed loudly against the walls and a small storm of dust fell from the floorboards as they moved across the room above. She held her breath, her ears straining to hear more. She heard a scrape like something heavy moving, then a small shuffling, then silence again.
She again concentrated on her breathing, struggling to quell the panic as it once again threatened to overtake her. Her heart thudded quickly in her chest, but she refused to give into the feeling, just breathe in and out she told herself.
Jim! Her foggy brain recalled, she had been with Jim, and they had been going... somewhere…

It was bright and sunny, she remembered, and they were driving. She remembered laughing at something he said and then the memory started to blow away like smoke.

The harder she tried to recall any details, the fuzzier the remembrance became.

The sound of footsteps above pulled away the last few tendrils of the thought from her memory. She listened as they crossed the floor above, and her heart stopped. The door she had noticed earlier opened. She closed her eyes and tried to relax. Some part deep in her mind told her it was better not to let this person who was now coming down the stairs know that she was awake.

The footsteps came slowly down the stairs and she fought the urge to peek as they descended. She heard the persons shoes shuffle on the floor and their steps as they drew closer to the table. She could hear the person breathing, long, slow, and deep as they stood over her.

She felt fingers on her head, poking and prodding some and seeming to study her scalp and it took everything in her not to scream in horror and pain. It felt as if they were digging into her very skull. The effort to be still, not respond, even to wince was superhuman.

She heard them move away, towards the workbench, and she heard the sounds as the person moved things about on it. Soft noises that she could not decipher. The footsteps shuffled back towards her and again her captor resumed the inspection of her skull.

She felt something cool on her scalp, a gentle touching and a rustling noise and a soft pressure. She felt it's fingers run along her cheek, down her neck and across her shoulder. The person traced their fingers along her arm and shoulder again and she could hear their ragged breath. The touch felt alien, cold, and appraising.
This was the worst part, even worse than the pain. This intimate touch, this violation. The flesh on her body crawled like the bugs you see scurry under rotted wood. She retreated deeper into her mind, trying to disconnect from any physical sensations to preserve her sanity.

Her memory from earlier returned as she submerged into herself. Her and Jim, driving, laughing. They had been on their way to the beach, she remembered that now, it was still early spring, and the roads were not yet crammed with the traffic that would magically appear after Memorial Day. She was happy and excited. They didn't have much time for each other lately and had planned this day to share some quality time.

Something had happened during the drive, something she couldn't recall, something bad.

Her next memory was of being in the woods, running.

She remembered looking back, seeing Jim running too, but he was covered in blood. She remembered screaming and almost falling, something running in her eyes, running her hand across her forehead and seeing the blood on her fingers.

They were being chased, something was behind them and she heard it coming. She looked back again and saw the fear on Jim's face and heard him scream.

"Just run Lori! Keep running!"

The sound of footsteps going up the stairs brought her back to herself with a start. She glanced over in time to see a pair of work boots and the bottom of a pair of jeans disappear through the closing door.
She felt her eyes well up at the thought of Jim. She wondered if he was OK, was he captured too, was he even still alive? Judging by her whereabouts, it didn't take a genius to guess they hadn't escaped from whoever it was that pursued them.

She shook off the feelings of despair the thought brought her, she closed her eyes again and did her breathing exercise, forcing herself to be calm. She was determined then, determined that she would escape.

She opened her eyes and slowly lifted her head. The pain was more nagging than sharp this time and she was able to look around clearly at her surroundings. She looked again at her left hand and pulled against the restraint lightly, gauging its strength. While cheap, it was still secure.

Looking to her right hand gave her a glimmer of hope. She had been wearing a bracelet on her right wrist. A large enameled piece that had been a gift from her sister Kay. She had bought it for her on their trip to the islands just a year ago and it had instantly become one of her favorite pieces. Her eyes welled up at the thought of her sister, and she wondered if she would ever see her again.

It was a larger bangle style bracelet, nearly an inch and a half thick and fit loosely on her wrist. Her abductor had made a mistake. He had placed the restraint over the bracelet rather than removing it. She turned her right wrist slowly and felt the bracelet slid on her wrist as well as the restraint.

Her breath stuck in her chest, she tucked the thumb on her right hand and slowly pulled up, trying to squeeze her hand from the bracelet and the restraint. She felt it slip up and onto the thickest part of her wrist. That was as far as she could get it. The angle her arm was at prevented her from pulling it up any further. She almost started crying as she tried to pull her wrist free. She placed her feet flat on the table, and pressed her elbows down, using her legs to try and push her body a few more inches up the table.
She froze as she heard noise from upstairs again, not even daring to breathe as she listened. Footsteps again, followed by a short metallic squeal like cheap furniture springs make.

She thought, "Yeah, relax you bastard, I'll be coming for you soon."
She managed to wriggle her body up a few inches, and this time as she pulled and twisted her wrist, the bracelet and restraint slid slowly then pulled over it and slipped easily over the rest of her hand.

She blew out a long slow breath, her whole body now covered in a gleam of sweat from the effort it had taken to free her one hand, her breath coming in short panting sounds like she'd been running. She only allowed herself a moment of rest though before struggling to sit up on her elbows to work on freeing her other wrist.

The world swam before her eyes when she sat up and the pain came back with a vengeance. She squeezed her eyes tightly closed and willed herself to stay conscious. After a few minutes, the pain subsided back to a dull roar and she was able to open her eyes again.

She managed to reach across and undo the other cuff from her left hand and pushing her legs off of the side, she stood shakily, holding tightly onto the table for support. Her vision clouded in and out with the thumping pain in her brain. She waited until she was as steady as she could be to move and started towards the workbench looking for some sort of weapon.

She found what she was looking for leaning against the wall to the right of the bench. An aluminium baseball bat. It was a dark flat gray. Black friction tape had been wrapped around its handle, now worn and faded, slightly unravelling and frayed at the end. Its barrel was pitted along its length and had a large dent on the one side that gave the bat a lopsided look.

Still, it felt right when she took it in her hand. She felt strong.
She stumbled slightly as she started to walk towards the stairs, catching herself on the table. She paused, her breath catching and she listened for any noise upstairs. She slowly started her journey again, being careful to be quiet.
She reached the bottom of the stairs, pausing to rest against the railing, her vision still hazy. She took a deep breath, forcing herself to be strong, and began the chore of climbing the steps.

She moved slowly, partially for stealth reasons and partially to keep her vision from greying out. She kept her feet to the sides of each step, trying to minimize the chance that the old wood of the stairs would creak.

A mixture of blood and sweat ran down her face, stinging her eyes. She blinked it away, pausing as she reached the top of the stairs trying to gather her strength.
She felt the determination build within her and she gripped the bat tighter, mentally psyching herself up, "I will not be a victim."

Her hand on the doorknob, she held her breath and turned it slowly, her ears perked for any noise from the room. She pushed the door open slowly, fractions of an inch at a time, pausing and listening.

She had the door open maybe an inch and she leaned forward and tried to see the room though the crack. The furnishings were neat, but sparse. She could see a couch and the back of a love seat coupled around an older console television to the right. Directly across from the door was an old China hutch that housed a few photos and some small knickknacks scattered on its shelves.

She couldn't see much to the left and had to open the door another inch before he came into view. She saw him, and her heart stopped. He was sitting at the desk, his back to her. He had his head down and was hunched over something he was studying. She could hear static swirling as if he were trying to tune in an uncooperative radio.

Her heart started beating again and she gripped the bat so tightly in her hand that her knuckles went white. Anger now joined her emotions directed at this person who had abducted her. She gathered her resolve, letting all of her emotions boil up inside of her and fuel her anger and want for revenge.

She squinted her eyes, trying to sharpen her vision. Her head throbbing in pain. She slowly pushed the door open enough to accommodate her slim body and slipped through into the room.

She raised the bat above her head as she crossed the short distance between them. He started to raise his head, but by then it was too late, the bat was already in motion.

She felt the bat connect with his skull with a satisfying thud. He went down off the chair and collapsed on the floor, blood spilling from the point of contact. She grabbed the desk for support, making sure he didn't move, the bat raised again just in case.

Her eyes searched the room, seeing the front door. She glanced down at the man at her feet, when she kicked at him and saw he didn't move, she stumbled past him and across the room.

She glanced back at him lying there, making sure he hadn't moved. Her hand twisted the front doorknob, pulled on it and found the door didn't budge. Brief panic engulfed her before she looked down and saw the deadbolt. She raised her hand to the thumb latch, turning and unlocking it. She opened the door, the bright sun blinding her.

Her heart sang as she went through the door and to freedom, slamming it shut behind her.

Jim sat at the desk and cried.
It wasn't fair, it just wasn't fucking fair.
He had saved her!
He had saved her from the crash and from the.. Zombies?
Whatever the fuck they were. They had caused the pile up on the road, and then brutally attacked the victims of the accident.

He had gotten her out of the car, she was half conscience, blood running in a flood down her scalp. She was confused and disoriented, but he had made her run. He got her to the house, got her in safely, even as those things pursued them. He could hear them hit the door seconds after he had bolted it closed.

He caught her at the door trying to unlock it as he was busy securing the house. She was in complete shock from the accident and the horror that followed. She fought him trying to get out the door, finally passing out in his arms as he held her tightly to him.

He had chosen to put her in the basement for safety. It was the most secure place in the house should those things manage to get in. He had grabbed his small travel bag as they ran from the accident mostly because it contained his gun, but it also held a cheap set of handcuffs he had brought along with more pleasurable thoughts in mind than what he was using them for now.

He had secured her to the table and checked her wounds. He was scared by the amount of blood she had lost. He went back upstairs and searched, finding a first aid kit in the bathroom. He had brought it down and tended to her wounds the best he could. Then he had come back up and was trying to find the news on the radio when she hit him.

His fingers lightly played over the lump on his skull from the bat. He had been awake enough to hear the door slam, then her screams started a moment later as "they" overtook her.

He finished the note he had been writing,

"Forgive me, I can't face this alone"

There were tears in his eyes.
It wasn't fair, he had saved her.

He brought the gun to his temple, his finger tightened on the trigger, and he went to join his love.

# # #

Peter Hartke

Peter Lives in a quiet town with his wife Tiffanna and their three dogs who are more like their kids.

The Genesis Man
by Luke Mepham

It seemed every person in town was in the supermarket on that particular Saturday morning. Every till had a cashier on them and every line had four to five people with deep trolleys queuing up. There wasn't a special occasion looming on the horizon. It was a hot and really humid day in the summer of 2014. Parents were becoming ignorant to the annoying whining of their children, who persist in screaming at the top of their lungs for no apparent reason.

John Fisher was on till number seven. That's the one with half of the buttons missing on the keyboard so he's been letting people walk away with free fruit. Nobody seems to give a damn though.

John looks around to see the crowded area by the returns desk, people moaning and swearing at whatever it was they didn't want. It's always like this but with an added sense of weirdness. He couldn't put his finger on it.

"Excuse me!" came a gruff voice.

John turned around and was met with a credit card up his nose. On the other end of the card was a very pissed off looking old man.

"Sorry sir. I'll just take that from you." John had a pain in his mouth. It was his tongue. He'd been biting it so he wouldn't give rude customers a piece of his mind. He needed this job. It was paying for his college fund. He'd taken a gap year to build up the money by going full time.

He's only got three more months before he can set off and say goodbye to this dead end job.

"Have a lovely day" he beamed a smile to the gruff voiced man who muttered something under his breath to John.

On the next till in front of his was a girl he'd taken a liking to. Her name was Charlotte and he'd only ever say Hello to her because of his shyness.

He looked at his next customer where a woman was balancing several children on her shoulders as if she was a set of monkey bars.

"Hi, any help packing?"

"Not now Daniel! Put it down Chloe!"

She wasn't up for a bit of chit chat, she had her hands full. The kids began screaming and John looked up, as he was scanning food, and locked eyes with Charlotte. She rolled her big brown eyes at him due to the kids and John just smiled and nodded.

John often imagined himself travelling through the earth's atmosphere towards space so he can escape the noise of this planet and find that quiet zone between here and there.
He moved his pen aside on the screen so he can see how long he had left. It wasn't good news as John let out a little groan. Four hours to go. He'd already been there three hours and that seemed like his whole shift. It was 11:59.

The customer had a few bottles of wine (He can see why), so he got out a cardboard box to put them in. It was one of those ones that just need a little squeeze and then it would all pop up into shape, but this is John and his luck was quite bad. Of all the thirty tills he had to be on the one with the crap wine boxes, one's that were covered in a bit of dust.

"Oh now that's dusty!" cried the woman.

"I can see that, ma'am" said John, trying to get it right.

"Remember the customer is always –

"Yes I do. I remember that."

The woman takes it from John and blows the dust into the air. But with this being John and his luck being bad, it all went and settled nicely into his nose hairs.

He's about to sneeze, the strong inhaling begins.

"I hope you brought a handkerchief, I don't want your germs" moaned the customer.

"ACHOOOOOOOO" – 'blip The clock had turned to 12:00pm.

The dust went everywhere and he managed to get some in his eyes. He went deaf momentarily. "Must've popped my ears" he thought.

He wipes his eyes and goes to scan the next item but it's gone. Everything has. He looks around and doesn't see anyone. The annoying customer with her children, queues of people, deep trolleys, co-workers, all gone. He reached up and pressed his ears and realized that he didn't pop them, but that everything just stopped and disappeared. The sound of tills beeping is now an echo. The food has all made its way back onto the shelves.

"That's weird" he said as if he was talking to anyone. He hoped somebody would just pop up and yell surprise.

"Okay everyone, I knew it was busy for no reason. Nice joke. I'm the fool. Who's the magician? You did that all within a split second. It's funny."
He comes out from behind the till and goes to Charlotte's to see if she was knelt down behind her desk. "Ha, it was funny Charlotte. I don't know what I did to deserve that. Charlotte?" She's vanished. Just like everyone else and, just like John began to think, maybe his sanity.

He walks up and down the aisles to the sound of his footsteps squeaking. He calls out various co-workers but with no answer. He goes downstairs to the staff cafeteria. Even the chefs are gone. No food out of the fridge, stoves turned off. He knocks on the store manager's door then laughs about it and just opens the door to an empty desk. He leans on the door and lightly bangs his head on it. He makes his way to his locker but doesn't expect to see anything in there. He punches his code in the locker and is surprised to see his backpack still inside. Everything is still in there, his drink, his sandwich and his phone. He takes the phone out to call his house and dials the number. A high pitched noise takes him by surprise. He drops the phone and it cuts out.

"What the hell is happening?"

He picks the phone up and looks at his recent calls. He made a mistake and pressed the wrong numbers, clearly. Except he didn't make a mistake and the number was correct. Every person has been wiped off from his phone list.

He takes his bag and runs back upstairs towards the front doors. Something catches his eyes and he stops in front of the Home department. All of the DVD's and CD's have no covers on them. They're just black cases. He turns his head outside to see the sun has gone behind thick dark clouds and has turned outside into a grey and draughty day. He goes outside and shivers. There's no birds, no cars, all of the trees are missing their leaves, like the flowers are missing the petals. He looks ahead of the car park towards the water fountain. It's the only thing out there that is making a noise. It's fully functional and working properly. John runs over to it and splashes his face. He cups his hand to drink some but spits it back out in disgust. Water is tasteless but what he just had in his mouth was as if the water had gone sour.

He looks back at the store and sees his bike, the only bike, still locked up. He runs to it and unlocks it and rides it through the town. It's windy but not cold. Like there's no air.
"Everything is still standing so it couldn't have been a nuclear bomb. If it was then what makes me so special?" he thought.

He approaches the Police Station and goes inside it. Just like the supermarket, everyone had disappeared. Even the cells were wide open with a new set of bedding on the bed.
"It's a dream. That's what it is, just a dream." He tries desperately to reassure himself but even he begins to doubt it.

John leaves the station and continues back on his journey to home. "Please be there Mum." He thought.

He turns the corner into his street and sees all of the cars in the driveways. He rides the bike over the front lawn of his house and jumps off from it and runs inside.

Once he's inside, he's met with the big picture frame that was hung in the porch next to the refrigerator. It held a picture of himself, his older sister, his Mum and his Dad in there. John's eyes begin to tear up. Of course that picture is what he wanted to see. He'd been seeing that picture for twelve years since it's been hanging there. Now it's just an empty frame. He dropped to his knees and began to cry. His head was in his hands and he was gripping his black hair. "What happened?" he muttered.

He stands up and throws the front door open, runs outside and screams at the top of his voice; "WHERE IS EVERYBODY?"

His tears have dried up and have left his eyes bloodshot.

He looks to his left and looks down at the rest of the street. The neighbor's house on the right side has a sprinkling system that starts to hiss over John. He blinks rapidly with every drop that hits his eyes. He gets up, wipes himself down and goes back inside.

He opens the fridge and sees all the food still in there but grey. It's like he was looking at a black and white television of a fridge. He picks up a gherkin and studies it. He takes a bite out of it and immediately spits it out. There's no taste, no smell. He goes to throw it at the wall but stops and looks at the gherkin. It has blobs of green on it from when he spat out. He sticks his tongue out to see if his tongue is now green, it's not. He goes to spit on the gherkin again but chokes himself out of saliva and ends up coughing. More green is going on it. He places it onto a plate and kneels down in front of it and then just breathes on it. The gherkin is now fully green. He picks it up and takes a bite out of it and success! The taste is back. He breathes on everything in the fridge and it turns back to its natural colour. At first he thought it was pretty nasty but if it brings the flavor back then it sure is worth it. He stops and begins to think that he breathed life into food. "What if I did that to clothes? Would it bring my family back?" He ran upstairs happy as ever, until he got to the bedrooms. There are no clothes in the drawers and no shoes under the bed.

He sits on the side of the bed. "I should just give up really." He scans the room and sees the phone book by his Dad's side of the bed. "There must be SOMEONE still out there." He grabs the book and flicks through the pages. All 1000+ blank pages.

He throws it down and begins to laugh at the circumstance.

"Hell, I'm the last guy on Earth. I can eat what I want, live how I want, do whatever I want." He starts to feel a slight of insanity but goes back to his bike anyway.

He rides through the town and back towards his work. When he gets there, he crashes his bike right through the front door. "Oh I'm sorry Officer but I really couldn't care less!" He laughs at his own clumsiness and looks towards the mannequins in the Home department. They're all faceless. John looks at the make-up and grabs some eye liner. He takes it to the doll's head and makes faces out of them. They look like bad drag queens but it makes him laugh.

"I'd take you out tonight, I'd rent a film but they don't exist anymore!" He notices one has a frown and he goes to fix it. "Aw now look at you".

Something clicked in his head. "At you – Atchoo, of course. I sneezed. If I go back to till seven and I sneeze, everything should come back! Oh John, you are a genius!"

He runs back to till seven armed with a pepper shaker. He sprinkles it on his nose and begins to get the feeling he's going to sneeze. He does. It echoed throughout the whole building. Sadly it was only the sneeze that John could hear. There were no customers ranting, no children screaming and no beeping from the tills.

John laughs and then stops abruptly. "Of course, you are a genius. With that kind of luck you can only spell negatively."

He walks slowly away from till seven with the buttons missing.

"I couldn't have died. This is something else. He talks out loud hoping somebody would hear him. "Well I guess there's nothing to live for. Why should everyone else have fun but me? I don't want to do what I want if there's nobody else to talk to, have a relationship with." He picks up the stem of a rose and breathes on it. It blossoms into a beautiful, big rose. He places it on Charlotte's till and walks out of the store.

He looks up and the tallest building in town, the cinema. It looms over him. He accepts his fate and goes to it.

He pulls down on the fire escape ladder and ascends the rungs one by one until he heard a noise. He stopped and listened out. 'Maybe just the wind' he thought, he continued up the ladder when he heard it again. He knew for sure that it wasn't the wind and he raced down the ladder and began shouting out.

"Hello is anybody there?" The noise happened again. He ran to the side of the cinema and the noise got louder. It's like somebody is crying.

'I'm not alone!' he thought.

The crying seemed to have a higher pitch than normal. John approaches what was making the noise and looks down at a basket.

"Oh my God" he muttered. The crying stopped. "A baby?" he managed to say.

The baby just looked up at John. He was wrapped in a blue blanket.

"Where did you come from?" He picks the basket up and the baby laughs at him. "Is your Mummy here? I can't tell you how nice it is to talk to a human being. I can't wait to meet her"
'Why am I talking to a baby?' he thought.

Another noise began coming from round the corner.

John's heart leapt out of his chest. "Is that your Mummy?" He ran around the corner whilst carrying the basket and stopped. The noise was more crying from what sounded like another baby.

John walked up to the other crying baby and this one was in a pink blanket. He took them both into the warmth of the cinema and placed the baskets on the floor.

He kneels down in between them and they have their eyes fixed on him.

"Now would be a good time for your first words, guys." They just continue gazing up at him. He stands up and walks around looking out of the screen doors to see if a woman is coming. He turns back to the babies and spots a note on the side of one of the baskets.

He picks the note up, hoping it will say 'Belated April Fool's Day!' or something macabre like that. With John's luck being bad, of course it doesn't say that. He does a double take at the note and seems confused by it. "Eve, what does that mean?" he said. That's when it dawned on him. He races over to the other basket with the baby wrapped in a blue blanket and looks for a note on it. He finds it and looks at the note. His heart stops and he tries to calm down. He looks down at the baby. "And your name is Adam". It was with that realization that John Fisher's luck was far from changing.

#

Luke Mepham

Luke Mepham is a writer born and raised in the West Sussex area of England. His interest in horror started when he was 6 after he watched Dawn Of The Dead late one night. Since then he was hooked. These days he is heavily influenced by anything horror and The Twilight Zone and in the stories he writes he enjoys to "pull the rug from beneath the readers". He has several short film scripts that have been made into films and feature length scripts that has caught the attention of filmmakers in Hollywood.

"I'm not easily scared but I do enjoy giving other people nightmares".

Something Old
*by **Belinda Kimmons***

Moira clung to traditions like a sailor adrift holding fast to a tattered lifesaver. If traditions weren't upheld, the world would drown in a sea of indifference, violence and chaos.

She tried to instill this sentiment in her children, fraternal twins Isolde and Ethan, until middle-school when they realized things were very different in their household. No other kids at school celebrated Yule, Hanukkah and Christmas, or Passover and Easter, or Halloween and Samhain as well as El Día de los Muertos.

Isolde and Ethan's dad Paul would simply fade into a semi-transparent state whenever Moira's rules about tradition were questioned. He enjoyed quite too much to complain or stand against her.

"I don't take sides."

Isolde and Ethan were fourteen when they decided it was time to break with Moira and her traditions. So they started with her self-imposed tradition of wearing Pilgrim costumes to the Thanksgiving table. While Moira was in the kitchen, Ethan and Isolde pleaded, "Dad. Please. Let us take these stupid things off. This isn't even a real holiday." But Paul shook his head.

He said, "I want to eat a good meal today kids. If you take the costumes off, your mother will become…disagreeable. You remember what happened on Halloween."

Moira had tossed out fifty dollars' worth of Halloween candy because Paul wouldn't wear the Druid costume for Samhain, carved a down curved mouth on the pumpkin instead of a smile "which was proper and traditional," and Isolde and Ethan switched Halloween costumes so he was the girl zombie and she was the boy zombie.
Before stomping up to her bedroom Moira, still in her Druid robes whirled on them, her eyes burning with anger, disappointment and betrayal. She screeched, "Halloween and Samhain are ruined!"

Paul, Isolde and Ethan rescued the candy in secret. Paul put on a black suit and a Freddy Kruger mask so the three of them could hang around outside giving Kit-Kats and mini-Snickers to the trick-or-treaters.

Paul was just too good of a guy. The kids found it physically impossible to be angry at him for long, so they settled into the Pilgrim costumes as best they could. The three of them stared silently at the Thanksgiving plates, a line of painted Pilgrims walking around the edges with little hatchets raised.

Isolde said, "She's crazy Dad. You know that, right?"

Paul scrubbed a hand over his face.

Ethan muttered, "If I had a hatchet, we could--"

Isolde whispered, "Stop it."

Paul adjusted the big black hat on his head and sighed. He said, "She just needs things to be a certain way. So please, for me, cooperate."

When the twins were eighteen, both of them prepared to go away to school. Ethan had stopped talking to Moira six months earlier. He entered a place that Moira said was 'dark and disturbing.' He didn't refute her assessment.
He told Paul, "It's easier. She leaves me alone. No traditions for this dark and disturbed teenager."

He resorted to twin speak with Isolde whenever Moira was nearby. Isolde tried to convince him to at least say good-bye before he left. He refused. Isolde went to university in Boston, Ethan in Chicago. Isolde returned after graduation. Ethan did not. He remained in Chicago for graduate school and whenever he phoned, he would only talk to Isolde or Paul.

Two years after graduation, Isolde moved out of the house in hysterics when Moira expressed interest in the obscure tradition of exsanguinations of chickens from a culture she couldn't recall, but was meant to bring prosperity and good things to the household. With the insistence of Ethan and the help of a therapist, Paul agreed to have her admitted to a hospital for thirty days of 'rest.'

The spring Isolde turned twenty-eight, she became engaged. Too much energy was required to dissuade her mother from plunging in, so Isolde let the wedding planning be Moira's drug of choice. She slept little, talked a lot and seemed to live on the hors d'oeuvres, wine and cake samples alone. They were sitting on the living room sofa after a day of dress-shopping, with stacks of wedding magazines, caterer menus and fabric swatches strewn about them like pastel leaves fallen from a big wedding tree.

Moira was in overdrive. "First, we need something old…something new… something borrowed…and something blue, and true to English tradition, a sixpence in your shoe. Isolde, honey, those things are imperative. I spoke to Mr. Cooper…you know, the antique guy?" gradually, Moira's voice went up several octaves. "He got me an authentic silver sixpence for you to put in your shoe!! When your father and I got married…"

At this point Isolde went into aural shut down so her mother looked like a silent movie actress going through the motions of speaking. A beep on her phone. Ethan. She read the text while Moira seemed to be talking about doves with ribbons tied to their ankles to be carried like a balloon bouquet.

Iz! Tell your mother I said tie tin cans to the wedding car. Luv u much. E.

The next day Isolde settled into the chair behind her desk at work. All the cubicles had short walls, so when the mail guy pushed his cart up to her cube and handed her a FedEx box, her cube neighbor leaned up from his chair.

"Oooo…a mystery box."

The box was from Ethan, and she made a little squeal before reaching for her letter opener. Tucked inside a cushion of Egyptian newspaper were two small lacquered wooden boxes, one black, and one red.

She whispered, "How lovely."

Beneath the tiny boxes was a reading copy of Ethan's latest book,
Odynophobia, Fear of Pain,
the next chapter in his bestselling series about victims' phobias that
turn out to be horrifically justified. She flipped to the dedication page.
'To I and P, who weathered the fear of madness and tradition.' The
small red card enclosed was covered in Ethan's square cramped hand.
She noticed he didn't capitalize Moira's name as if she was no longer a
unique entity.
Iz, sorry I can't make it. I'll be in Hong Kong for two weeks for the
book tour. Tell Dad I luv him. The red box is yours and the black box,
moira's. As tradition dictates, it's something old. One for each of you.
Luv u much. E.

Paul beamed when Isolde handed him the book. She thought his face
would break when he read the book's dedication. Moira flipped a
derisive hand at them. If she was hurt that Ethan didn't include her in
the dedication, she didn't show it. She called over her shoulder as she
headed down the hall to the kitchen, "Ethan's books are not traditional
literature, just a means to pander to the hoi polloi."

Paul whispered, "Hoi Polloi?"

Isolde and Paul sat on the sofa and she took the boxes out of her purse.
First she opened the tiny red box and on a small square of white velvet
was a gold brooch. The symbol looked like a staircase that was large at
its top and tapered at its lower end. Engraved on the back was a tiny
word. "Djed."

Isolde said, "Ethan told me about this. It's the Egyptian symbol for the
human backbone and represents stability and strength."

She opened the tiny black box and sitting on red velvet, was a hand
carved brooch of white stone. Paul adjusted his glasses.

"What is that? Alabaster?"

"I don't know. This is Mom's gift. Looks like a vase with a bouquet of
curved flowers. And I think that's a bird. Look."

She turned the brooch so he could see. There was a note stuck into the top of the box that she picked at with her pinky until it popped out. Written in beautifully formed letters was 'The Two Ladies.' Ethan didn't write this.
"Two ladies?"

Paul shrugged. "Don't give it to your mom now. Wait until she can't...you know, react."

Moira called from the kitchen, "Lasagna's ready."

Isolde remembered Ethan's earlier note and called back, "Ethan told me to tell you that he really, really wants us to tie tin cans to the wedding car!"

There was silence for nearly a minute before Moira called back.

"Oh I am sorry dear. Shoes are better traditionally. They represent good luck."

On the morning of the wedding Isolde, her bridesmaids and Moira were in Isolde's old bedroom, fussing over her hair, makeup and dress. She carefully pinned the gold brooch from Ethan right below her bodice. After asking the girls to give them a moment, she took the other brooch from its box and pinned it to Moira's yellow dress, near her heart.

"Oh…" Moira whispered, "How lovely…"

"It's from Ethan Mom. He said, 'as tradition dictates.' We both have something old."

Reflexively, Moira reached for the pin to remove it, but stopped. The white stone was smooth and milky and warm to the touch, as if alive. Moira was briefly transfixed.

Isolde said, "The figures on it are called The Two Ladies."

Moira admired the brooch in the mirror and murmured, "Finally. He understands tradition is vital to the balance of things."

The wedding car drove slowly away from the church dragging old boots and shoes behind it. The couple turned around so they could be seen in the back window waving to the crowd still tossing rice in their direction. After the reception, Dad and Moira returned home, exhausted. Moira kicked off her dressy sandals, and Dad waved off a cup of tea to go to bed.

She stood at the kitchen counter and sipped her tea, but her insides were buzzing too much. Still in her mother-of-the-bride dress, she made her way through the dark to the den so she could e-mail people about the success of her wedding planning. She frowned at the screen. There was an email from Ethan with the subject "Something Old." She stared for several seconds, deciding. Read, or delete. Read, or delete. She sighed and clicked on the email.

"I assume you're wearing my little gift. I got it from an antiquities dealer in Cairo. Believe it not, it was carved nearly a thousand years ago. The images represent The Two Ladies, Wadjet the snake goddess and Nekhbet the white vulture goddess, protectors of ancient Egypt."

Moira looked down at the brooch. She looked back at the screen.

"Unlike Egypt, we—me, Dad, and Isolde—didn't have the snake goddess or the white vulture goddess to protect us from you and your craziness with those fucking over-the-top traditions. Chicken blood, moira? Remember that? But I'm making fucking sure Isolde's kids will be protected."
The message ended that way.

She whispered, "On drugs."
Suddenly, another email from Ethan popped up on the list. She clicked on it.

"I almost forgot. When I said to tie tin cans to the wedding car, I knew you'd choose shoes. But the tradition of tin cans tied to the wedding car was originally to ward off spirits. And I couldn't have that. I had to be sure The Two Ladies were free to do their job. You'll see."

Moira tish-tosh and deleted the emails, shutdown the computer and headed to the stairs. She looked down at the polished parquet steps and decided she would run a dust mop over the stairs in the morning. She was humming as she ascended slowly, but on the third step she felt a pin prick above her left breast. Thinking the fastener on the brooch came loose, she squeezed the thing to close it, went up another step.

There was another pin prick but deeper, enough to draw a tiny bead of blood. Moira grabbed the brooch, tried to unfasten it to pull it off her dress but the thing wouldn't budge. Five more pinpricks followed. She attempted to call her husband, but fear constricted the muscles in her throat.

That's when her gaze skirted past the blood trickling down her chest, to the brooch. The fastener wasn't pricking her. The ten tiny carved flowers were moving. They were making holes in her skin. Sudden realization screamed at Moira that they were not flowers at all. Cobras? Ten cobras fanned out like a bouquet. She thought, the brooch won't come off, the dress will. She tried frantically to rip the material but couldn't. Ten pin pricks, then twenty, then thirty, each deeper than the last.

The cobras grew larger as they undulated from the confines of the brooch. Their hooded heads snapped back and forth like needles in a sewing machine, perforating her skin until it looked as if there was a zipper in her chest. Moira wanted…needed…to scream as gradually, her skin split open to reveal the muscle beneath which in turn split open to expose the bone. Her mouth stretched wide but no sound escaped. Red-black blood poured from her chest, saturated her dress, dripped from its hem, and pooled on the bottom three steps. Panic and the excruciating pain were shutting down coherent thought, but Moira, operating on instinct alone, wrapped her hands around the rail to her right. Her bare feet made a high-pitched skirling over the blood-slick parquet as she attempted to get up the stairs.

She couldn't get a sufficient grip on the rail to go farther, the blood having coated her hands to her fingertips. She slid backward while scrambling to hold on to anything, and fell flat on the floor at the foot of the staircase. The back of her head slammed against the parquet causing her consciousness to blink in and out.

In slow motion a tiny white eagle, no…god no…a white vulture emerged from the brooch, its body expanding, growing until it was fully grown; a white feathered devourer of carrion.

When it reached the ceiling, it circled once above her, its huge wings extended, its body tilted at an angle, ready to strike. The vulture waited, turning its head so it's yellow T-Rex eyes could watch chest gradually slow. It watched until her muscles no longer twitched..

The vulture swooped down, hopped around the body, and flapped its enormous wings to fend off any interlopers though there were none. And by tradition, the vulture lowered its head, and did what it was created to do.

#

Belinda Kimmons

Belinda Kimmons was born when rotary phones were still in use, and Superman could change in a phone booth. She retired after over twenty years as a civil servant. Since she retired, she spends hours ripping ideas out of her brain.

She has been writing something or other that was strange or creepy for a long time. Apparently the stories were creepy enough to invoke sufficient fear in one friend who admitted she was actually afraid to meet Belinda in person (which pleased her immensely). Writing was a hobby and she never considered publishing until her loving friends kicked her in several places with their collective boot.

The Preacher
*by **Vardan Partamyan***

He did not know how he survived. On that day an eternity ago there was the choir and the mass and the believers seeking refuge in the only place that was beyond logic, beyond the bad news on television, beyond the fear and the panic and feeling of impending doom. They came to the church to hear him speak the words of wisdom, to give them hope and a glimmer of salvation. And he was prepared to give it – his voice was strong, his eyes clear – he was clearly having a blast, lost in the holy texts he even didn't notice how much brighter the chamber looked, the shudder of the earth and the silence. It was only when the windows blew in that he snapped back to reality to see his parish swept away, the benches flying and fire storm raging all around him.

He stood mesmerized and shocked and totally unhurt. Everything moved in slow motion and so did he, he slowly descended from the altar, crossed the church walking among the dead – people who had come there for him to save them, people whom he had let down. And still he walked on, the fire touched him not. He went out of the building and the hell was upon earth and the ground was burning and the houses were swept away and the screams of the living echoed by the silence of the dead. He couldn't blink and his eyes were wide open and he could not see for seeing was believing and he couldn't believe what was going on. And so he walked on through the fire and death and the devastation and into a tunnel that lead down. A tiny part of his mind that was still trying to rationalize had no idea what the place was, had no idea why the priest was still alive or how did he know where to go. That tiny part of his mind screamed and protested and begged to go back and die with everything else but something pushed him on and on and to a large metallic door with green digits burning in darkness. He punched in the code. What code?- the part of his mind screamed? And the huge door opened and he stepped inside and it was dark and the door closed behind him and the lights came on and he was safe and immediately unconscious. He came to hours or days or years later to first question what really happened, then disbelieve what he remembered, then understand that disbelieving was done with, then walk around the place he was in only to discover huge supplies of food and water and plants growing under artificial light and no one else at all. And so his new life started just as the old one was annihilated in that other world where he was the preacher and the savior and the voice of the good.

In his new life his only friends were the plants and the books he found and there were worlds undiscovered that were a wonder to him and he shared that wonder with his friends never once doubting that he was completely and utterly insane and there would come a moment when his brain would simply cease to function and he would be blissfully dead and gone just as he should have. Time passed and he lived on and as his new life moved on, he found peace in the silence, wisdom in the simple plant and joy in breathing the air and simply being alive. For many years he lived enclosed in the shell of the military vault that failed to save any military personnel. He had lost the count of the days and years he was there. His hair turned white, his face grew wrinkled and hard. And yet he felt serenity and was, in a way, the happiest person in the world – if there even was such place as world. Then one day it all ended. His peaceful existence was shattered by the roar of the sirens and warnings uttered in pre-recorder female voices. They were screaming about decompression and evacuation and self destruction and giving him a deadline of fifteen minutes to get out or face disciplinary action. Get out? Where to? The images of the burning parish sprang before his eyes and he closed them and they were still there imprinted deep into his brain, into his body that was supposed to die with everyone else but did not. And so he walked, taking nothing with him but the clothes he wore and he went out of the door he entered all those years ago and he was outside – in the desert that was his town in the life before. His travels began and he met the people and he talked to them and they recognized him for who he was and he gained their respect and admiration and there were many things he would tell those lost souls of the apocalypse – many things they wanted to and so believed in. The one thing he did not tell them was that he himself no longer believed – his faith was dead just as he was supposed to be dead, just as this world was supposed to be dead.

# # #

Vardan Partamyan
Vardan Partamyan was born in Yerevan, Armenia, in 1983. After returning from studies in the US, he enrolled in the Yerevan State University - majoring in Political Science and English language. In the

years that followed, he was an author of and contributor to a number of non-fiction publications mainly dealing with the issues and challenges facing his newly independent country. Writing fiction has been a long time passion/obsession for Vardan who mixes influences from writers such as Stephen King, J.R.R. Tolkien, Harry Harrison, Alfred Bester, Ernest Hemingway and Ian Fleming with the eternal themes of a man's strive for freedom, the quest for self discovery and the knowledge of the unknown, presented on the backdrop of sometimes fantastical surroundings and events.

An Unholy Halloween
*by **Robert A. Read***

My appearance may be misleading if you are unaware of my story. From the wispy feathers of white hair, the gaunt features and wrinkled parchment yellow skin, you may think my age to be near eighty years. In fact my true age is less than half that total. I am entirely to blame. If I had paid more attention to the warnings from the local villagers...

In the three autumn seasons through which I have lived in this tiny, Devonshire village on the edge of Bodmin Moor, I have never been visited by the local children on All Hallows Eve. I realize that 'trick-or-treat' is more of an American theme, but in the last twenty years or so, it has become almost as popular here in England.

The first two years were understandable; I needed to earn the villagers' trust. My little thatch-roofed cottage set among surly horse-chestnut trees and away from the main road was a little creepy. That fact, added to the suspicion of a middle-aged man living alone, and with stories of sex-offenders and paedophiles making almost daily headline news, how many parents would be willing to allow their precious offspring to come near my abode?

However, by the third year, I was on first name terms with all my immediate neighbours. They knew by then, that being an artist, I had an excuse for a little eccentricity. Several of my better paintings hung on the walls above the bar of the quaint little pub, the Red Lion, and I had received requests from two of the patrons for portraits of their young ones which I completed from photographs they supplied.

Through the harvest season of that year and the next, I received gifts of home-grown vegetables from, at least, four families, which I repaid by allowing their older children to collect apples and plums from my small orchard. I was therefore, even more surprised to have no costumed revellers standing on my doorstep through that last night of October. My fourth Halloween was the time I decided to show them I was happy to become involved in the yearly festivities. The shop windows of the stores in the nearest town were filled with the masks, costumes and trinkets to which we have become accustomed, almost from the end of summer. The week before the end of October, I purchased half a dozen plastic jack-o-lanterns, several cut-out, broomstick riding witches and black cats, and felt almost ready to entertain.

These items, displayed on the trees and walls of the house, I hoped would attract the village children. I also bought a supply of sticky sweets and chocolate goodies to hand out in the best Halloween tradition.

The night before All Saints' day, while sitting in the bar of the Red Lion, I noticed that Pete, the landlord of the house had made no attempt to add seasonal decoration. The half-timbered walls and dark stained low wooden beams were made for a touch of Gothic horror.

"Do you not celebrate Halloween?" I asked him.

The moment I mentioned the time of year, a cloying hush fell over the ten or so drinkers. I felt their searing gaze burning into me. For a moment, I thought I had spoken some profane blasphemy.

Lowering my voice I added, "I ask because I've never seen children trick-or-treating like they do in the towns."

"You'll not see such tom-foolery celebrated in these parts. Maybe those city dwellers have nothing to fear with their bright lights, but here the night when the dead walk abroad is a night we fear most deeply."

"Oh, come-on," I said. "It's only a bit of fun. A few sweets for children in fancy costumes."

"It's the one night of the year we keep our doors firmly barricaded. If any children come a knocking on your door my friend, you will be well advised to keep it firmly locked. Now I will be obliged if you make no more mention of this"

His manner and that of his customers unnerved me as I walked home that evening, but passing several houses with candle-lit lanterns in the windows, I put his reticence down to the likelihood that a night of partying would reduce his weekly profit margin.

The following evening, as darkness fell, I hung the lighted lanterns at the entrance to the porch of the house. I had already nailed the witches to the trees on the driveway from the road so that they pointed like direction arrows to my door. With sweets and chocolates displayed in bowls on a low table inside the porch, I waited.

I waited in vain for what must have been four hours. Several times, I went outside in the hope of seeing moving lights or figures under the street lamps. There seemed no sign of a living soul. By ten-o'clock, with wisps of cold mist drifting between the leafless trees, I came to the conclusion that this was another wasted Halloween. I closed the door, leaving the candles in the lanterns to burn themselves out, stoked up the log fire and settled down to read.

I must have slipped into a state of sleep from the warmth of the fire, before I was startled into wakefulness from a sudden noise. I jerked upright in the chair as my book fell with a thump onto the carpet. Apart from the ticking of the clock on the mantle there was only silence through the house. I was still trying to work out if it was imagination that had woken me when the same sound resolved into a tapping on the front door.

A visitor at such a late hour was most unusual. I was concerned as to who would call at this time. The door of my lounge opens onto the porch, the outer door of which, I remembered having left open to the night air. Moving quietly to the door, I pressed my ear against the wood for any sound that might identify my visitor. I believed I could detect faint whispering voices the way children whisper in classes when they should be studying.

I had an uncomfortable feeling, laced with fear. Whatever would children be calling for at this time. The clock indicated it was past eleven. Then I remembered the Halloween inviting lanterns pointing their way to my door. Of course! But still, this was much later for trick-or-treat than I expected.

At that moment, I regretted having no safety chain or peep-hole in the door. As I debated the predicament in my mind, another gentle tap caused me to jump in alarm. I was certain I heard the tiniest giggle from the other side of the door. It had to be two or more children calling for their trick or treat goodies.

Steeling myself, I reached out for the door handle. A small voice in the back of my mind urged me most vociferously not to open the door. But it was only children. What could be the harm in letting them have some of the chocolate treats?

I convinced my nervous state into believing the fear could be no more than due to waking so suddenly. I turned the doorknob. The door emits a creaking groan if opened slowly as in the best traditions of haunted houses. My intention was to use the effect to scare my visitors before I would step from the shadows like some ghastly ghoul.

As the entrance came into view the surprise hit me. I stared!

On the stone step stood a child, a girl of no more than ten years. She wore no mask, but she was made up to look the part. With long dark hair and pallid skin, I guessed she was meant to be a vampire. What caused me the astonishment was her attire. Dressed only in a white, short-sleeved smock that fell below her knees she must have been freezing. The garment may well have been a nightdress from my limited knowledge. Her hands were clasped across her stomach, and she clutched a raggedly dressed, china doll, while gazing at a point on the floor in front of her.
Bedraggled and dripping moisture, I could believe she had come in from the rain. Perhaps the mist had thickened since I had been inside. Behind her stood two more children, a boy and a girl dressed in similar gowns. Several years younger, these two could have been twins from their similar appearance

I looked into the moonlit night for a parent I could admonish for letting children wander the streets in such a state. There was no one in view. I opened my mouth to speak, but no sound could I utter as the girl looked up at me.

Shock hit me as if I had been thrown into an icy river. Her eyes, staring unblinking at me were large and black as a piece of jet. Entirely black, yet alive, glistening from the reflected light of my lounge.

I stepped back as she spoke. I was expecting her to say, 'Trick or treat.' The voice was hoarse as if from a sore throat. The words that came from her were, "Feed me!"

The other two shuffled forward into the light. Their eyes, totally black like the girl's gazed at me as they echoed, "Feed me."

A sensation came as of an icy hand gripping my throat and I could not prevent a shudder running through my body. "I have some chocolate which..." My tongue struggled to form the words.

"So, so cold," she continued. "Let us in. Feed us."

I was almost numb with an uncontrollable fear, yet I tried to think logically, they are only poor children. How could I refuse a little charity? I stepped back to allow them entry.

The events that preceded my awakening in hospital, I had no recollection. Apparently, a neighbour found me the following morning. He said that the door was open, and, with no response to his knock, he had entered. I was sitting in the chair before a fire that had long since gone out. Apparently, I was babbling about evil, dead children and not even knowing their names.

That is my story. You may believe it or not as you like. They say this is an old peoples' home, and that I am not capable of looking after myself. I feel like a prisoner. I am certain, although the doctors will not admit, this is a mental asylum. They treat me reasonably well, but I feel the eyes of the other inmates burning me with contempt.

The children? They took nothing from me – nothing in any physical form that is. They took nothing other than forty years of my life.

# # #

Robert A. Read
Originally from south-west of England, the author now resides in Burgundy, France with a small army of feral cats. A writer of short stories and novels, he adheres to no particular genre, although much of

his writing depicts elements of the occult & paranormal. He also write a little poetry, usually on dark subjects, but never considers himself to be a poet, likening it more to weaving colourful patterns with words on a form, which hopefully depict an image to the reader like a tapestry.

Something In The Blood

*by **Saul Hudson***

They're getting closer. So close. God knows I left them enough clues. My name is Frank Morgan, thirty five, and you'll only ever have known me as The Child Catcher. It's a strangely apt name, suitable for the likes of me, I'm sure you'll admit, but it is a title that I look upon with a certain kind of relish. Nobody has ever remembered me so well, not even in school. I'm just plain old Frank nothing special, nothing memorable, and nothing worth a shit in modern society. But I'm different in so many ways that make other people, normal people I guess you could say; think about me with a sickeningly sour taste in their mouths. Undoubtedly if they ever find me they'd be inclined to lynch me from the nearest lamppost. And I wouldn't blame them.

I could try and explain how none of this was my fault, or how the real fault lies within my basic makeup done since my conception. I could even blame my father for beating me too much or my mother for never allowing me suckle on her teat until I was tired – but that would be a cop out . . . I am what I am because something inside me demands it of me. And if you can accept that you are halfway there to accepting who I really am.

First and foremost I am a killer – cold and calculating all the way – and secondly I am The Child Catcher: I kill, rape, and torture girls before leaving their bodies somewhere they would be easily found without a trace of me left behind. I'm careful and fastidious in what I do - the perfect craftsman if ever there was one.

I live alone in a modest detached house, the curtains always drawn, no lights ever burning in the lower windows except for the bedrooms above, I don't even step out of the house for groceries until nightfall. It is, by all accounts, an unimpressive dwelling left to rot behind thick weeds and rampant grass, the number on the door rusted over and veiled by silk webs spun over long periods of time. From time to time I will hear people in the front yard but I never chase them away . . . where is the science in chasing them away?
By and large, however, they leave me to my darkness, daunted by the ramshackle appearance of the house than my occupancy. I'd long since

been forgotten about by the world – nobody came and nobody went, and if I were to die in my sleep I doubt anyone would notice.

But I digress. I want to tell you about Sarah Higgins as it will be my last testimony to the world before my trial (if I am not murdered beforehand). I'm not sure how old she was, perhaps thirteen at the very least but it is so hard to tell these days, but she was the sweetest of them all.

She came to my door sometime before noon the week of Friday 22nd of August dressed in a black pleated skirt that rose a good ten inches above her knees in a white blouse that seemed molded around her pert breasts. Her hair was tied into pigtails, pulled tight either side of her head, and her face was full of the cutest freckles I'd ever seen. She spoke courteously and asked if I would make a donation to the children's fund for which she was collecting. It was impossible for me to say no.

We debated on the front step for a while, as was my method of choice, and I asked her inside as I looked for my wallet. Unsurprisingly she followed me inside, peering in and out of the adjacent rooms without so much as a peep. I am not sure what made me put the chloroformed rag over her mouth no more than you could tell me why you do the things you do, except to say I did it because the moment took me . . . I wanted to know what she looked like inside as well as out. Killing her was more than just spilling her out at my feet.

The cellar is no more than thirteen feet by thirteen feet in either direction. The cobble looking walls are damp and spotted with moss in places and a water pipe drips incessantly into a bucket because I haven't had the time or money to have it fixed. A single bulb burns in the centre of the room shedding shadows along the walls and over the single mattress I occasionally let my tenants use. But in the centre of the room, hanging from a wooden beam, were the shackles that little Sarah would eventually hang from. I stripped her naked, shackled her, and splashed cold water on her face until she came around.

As with some of my previous work, I never raped her, the thought far from my mind. Instead I circled her like a cat stalking its prey, my fingers occasionally tracing a thin line over her flesh with jittery nervousness. Once or twice I felt her flinch, the way they all did in the beginning, her flesh crawling against mine in complete utter revulsion.

"Such a sweet girl." I said as much to myself as her. "So sweet."

I occasionally stood in front of her, gazing her up and down, tracing yet another nervous finger over her forming breasts and down her stomach until her legs clamped together around the delicate mass of pubic hair.

"What do you want?"

The question was so absurd and obvious that I laughed.
"Don't worry about the details . . . I want you to enjoy the moment while you have it. Enjoy the feeling of another person's touch . . . flesh against flesh . . . married in a perfect union." "I want to go home! I want to go home to my mum!"

"There are such things I could show you? I could teach you everything and deny you nothing." I ran my fingers through her hair, watching my own reflection in her widening eyes as I was looking into a mirror. "Don't fight me, Sarah, you'll thank me for it later." "Let me go!" "Don't fight it, you'll only make it worse for yourself." I whispered into her ear, the tip of my fingers touching the crease of her sex.

"I'll scream! If you don't let me go right now I'll scream!"

"Then scream . . . who do you think will hear you?"

I punctuated the point myself by letting out a harrowing scream of my own - the kind of scream I learnt to hold in when my father came into my room at night when my mother had gone to work. She joined the chorus until she was horse and gagged on her dry throat. I opened my arms as if to bow to her, and said: "See, didn't I tell you it was pointless?"

"Why are you doing this to me?"

I circled her again. "Maybe this was what you were born for. Has nobody ever told you that every single person has a reason for being born? That there is some greater plan for all of us? You were born for this moment, conceived for this, and you didn't even know it."

"Let me go!"

"We were brought together. It was designed from the beginning, and whether you understand or accept it isn't any real concern to me. All that matters is that destiny brought you here and destiny will take you out of here. Simple, isn't it?"

Between the tears and escalating protests she tried to free herself by jerking her whole body against the shackles. They were never going to give way, not in a million years, but the sight of her breasts moving up and down in time to her aggravated motion gave me such a hard on.
I watched her for three days, allowing her nothing more than bread and water to sustain her – and it was from within the shadows that I watched every ounce of humanity ebb out of her. Eventually she would give in to me (they always do) but during the interim I was content in watching from the shadows.
She gave up hope of rescue shortly after the third day. It wasn't hard to understand why every scream and shout had fallen upon deaf ears. Once in awhile I heard her mutter something just beyond the realms of audibility, a prayer perhaps, before sinking once more into silent despair.

As was my custom, I masturbated in the final moments. Inside the shadows I imagined myself crawling over her, conjuring the sensation of flesh against flesh, the smell of sex soaking us both, and at the very peak of my climax I stepped out of the shadows to face her and tarnish her dry flesh with my salt. Afterwards I reached for my old knife, wrapping my hand around the wooden shaft softly, and the blade would glint against the single bulb that burnt over both our heads.

I didn't kill her for another thirty minutes.

I beat and punished her for every imaginable sin. I cannot recall now the exact sins, they seem to slip my mind as soon as they're atoned for, but I remember the exact sequence in which I dealt my punishments. Firstly; I broke her jaw with a single punch, the bone snapping loudly and clearly in the confined space. Secondly; I slashed at her breasts, almost completely shedding the nipples from her chest with the first blow, then moving on down her abdomen until her stomach was a crisscross of slashes. She screamed, of course, as much for her broken jaw than the hairline scratches left by the blade. Thirdly; and the last of all the punishments, I skinned her back almost completely.

She was almost dead by third punishment – the screams had long since past. Once in awhile her body jerked, her eyes dulled by pain as they rolled back into her skull, but she never stopped fighting against the shackles. Eventually, I slit her throat and bled her over a green bucket until her veins ran dry.

I spent two days disposing of her remains, filling black bags with torn arms and legs before booting the remains into the trunk of my car. I'll ditch the parts at night and listen to the distant sound of sirens, and I will wonder, like I always do, just how long it will take them to find me.

I occasionally wonder if I would like to be something else: a banker, a realty broker, or, simply, the man next door with three point two children and a wife who smiles adoringly every day, and do you know what?, I could be any one of those things right now – I could even be the guy who calls you down for dinner if I wanted.

#

Saul Hudson

Saul lives with his daughter in a quiet little town in the middle of England. He has appeared in numerous anthologies and is currently working on putting the finishing touches to his forthcoming novella Season of the wolf.

The Cats

by James G. Kelly

Ricky and Robin Kelsey had been married for eight years. All the while they had been looking for that perfect house. They had found a few that they could afford but none of that felt right. They didn't feel at home in any of them. One day while riding home from work Ricky saw a sign on the main road of a house for sale and decided to check it out. It was an old house in need of repairs, but it felt right. He hurried home to the one room apartment they had been living in and picked up Robin and took her to see the house. She could tell from his excitement that this may be the one.

Robin loved the little one story rancher as much as Ricky. It was in a small neighbourhood just a few blocks off the main road. The small copse of woods behind the house gave it that country feel while still being close to the city and stores and Ricky's job.

After acquiring the house Ricky began the repairs on the outside while Robin worked her decorating magic on the inside. Only one month later they stood back and looked at the finished product. White paint for the siding, trimmed in green and a new roof over the deck styled front porch and the place looked great. They were finally home.

All was fine for the first few years they lived in the house. The neighbours were friendly enough and had even thrown a little get together to welcome them to the neighbourhood. Then one day a black cat appeared in the front yard. Ricky yelled at it to go away, but the cat ignored him. It was a sleek, black tom with piercing yellow eyes. He was sitting on his haunches under the holly tree in the front yard staring at Ricky as he sat on the front porch. Ricky got an eerie feeling from the cat. After all black cats were big in superstition as being familiars for witches and also bad luck if one were to cross your path. What did that say about one that stayed in your path?

Ricky didn't blame Robin, but she is the one who started it all by feeding that black menace. She would throw scraps out for him, which Ricky didn't mind because she would have thrown them away anyhow. Blackie, as she called him, would gobble them up as if he hadn't eaten in weeks, but he seemed healthy and strong. Not one bone showed through his muscular physique.

Ricky loved sitting out on the porch watching the neighbours go by and waving to them while enjoying the fresh air. The cool breezes of spring and fall were wondrous and even the summers weren't so bad thanks to the shade cast by the holly tree. The winters could be a little harsh, but even that didn't deter him from sitting outside watching the children play in the snow. They would build snowmen and have snowball fights; ride their sleds down the hill, barely missing the trees at the bottom of the hill where the road turned sharply left. The kids had one or two days of sledding before the plows would come through and clear the road.

Every time Ricky would come outside to enjoy his cigars, Blackie would sit under the holly tree and stare at him; stare with those yellow eyes, and it wasn't a pleasant look. It was a "I'm going to get rid of you" look. It became quite unnerving for Ricky after a while, but Robin thought he was being stupid. It was just a cat. Ricky understood Robin's feelings because Blackie's expression would change whenever she was around. His expression would become soft and loving when directed at her.

Soon one cat became two, then three, they just kept coming. Scraps were no longer enough to feed the darned things and Robin had to start buying food for them. That wasn't what bothered Ricky. What bothered him was the fact that they all would sit on their haunches under the holly tree and stare at him. It got to the point where there were so many of them he started to actually fear for his safety. He felt as though they were plotting his death as they stared at him.

Ten, fifteen then twenty, it seemed as if a new one would show up every day. Robin is right they're just cats, he thought. There were cats of all shapes and sizes and colors. Even the kittens that are supposed to be so cute would sit with the others and watch his every move. Robin felt that Ricky was being paranoid, but she didn't see them looking at him with those horrid cat eyes as they rubbed against her legs. She didn't notice them edging towards him as he walked to the car. It was him they didn't like; him that they seemed to want out of the way.

Then things started to happen. Ricky came out one morning and tripped over a toy car that had been left on the steps and broke his arm as he tried to catch his fall. Robin suggested one of the neighbourhood kids had left it there, but he knew it was those darned cats.

After the incident, and against Robin's wishes, Ricky began to set traps for the cats. He was determined to rid his yard of the horrid beasts. A week went by and not one trap had been sprung. The cats were too smart for that. Desperate to get rid of the cats, Ricky sat out poison for them. He would mix it in with their food after Robin went back into the house after feeding them, but they wouldn't go near it.

A few weeks later the temperature dropped well below the freezing mark. Robin filled the pet's water bowls with fresh water before she went to bed. The next morning Ricky came out to go to work and almost broke his neck as he slipped on the ice patch right in front of the door. It had to be a deliberate act and of course Ricky blamed the cats.

"Jim, those cats are going to kill me," Ricky told his coworker one day at work.

"C'mon Ricky, you sound paranoid about those stupid cats. They can't kill you. They may scratch you pretty bad, but they can't kill you," said Jim with a bit of a chuckle.

"Well, you're not there; you don't see the way they look at me."

"Can you explain to me how they could kill you?"

"I don't know Jim, it's just a feeling I have. You know things aren't the same between me and Robin either. She thinks I'm going crazy. She always sides with the cats over me; over my feelings."

"She's not the only one, Ricky. You are not sounding like a sane man to me either. Why don't you try and get rid of them?"

"Believe me I've tried. Traps, poison I've tried everything. They will not fall for any of it."

"What about animal control?"

"I thought of that as well, but Robin said she would kick me out if I tried that one. She has fallen in love with them. She gives those darn cats more attention than she does me."

Ricky went to bed early after an unusually tiring day at work. He woke up shivering and noticed that the window had been left open. He got up to close it and tripped over something falling to floor. It was a cat. They had torn the screen and climbed in through the window. It wasn't just one, they were all in there. They began to claw and scratch him as he tried to make it to the door by crawling along the hardwood floor. He felt the cats biting him as he tried to throw them off, but there were too many of them. They were tearing at his flesh and biting into his neck while he struggled as best as he could against the attacks. He was about to pass out from lack of blood when beep, beep, beep.

Ricky awoke in a sweat as he looked around for the beasts. Then he settled a bit and turned off the alarm. It had been a dream, but it had seemed so real. Robin couldn't hold back a chuckle as Ricky related the nightmare to her. He didn't find it the least bit funny and was still a little shaken as he went to take a shower.

After a couple of weeks of no incidents from the cats, Ricky noticed that they seemed to have a different look about them as he left for work one morning. It was almost as if they were smiling. He thought that perhaps they were instituting some kind of a truce with him. Maybe they were finally starting to like him, or at least tolerate him. After all that had happened he would be glad to end the hostilities with the cats. It had become a war he felt he couldn't win.

He didn't think any more about it as he started the car and headed down the steep hill that made such a great sledding hill in the winter for the children. Nearing the bottom of the hill where the road turns sharply to the left, Ricky hit his brakes and the pedal went to the floor. It was impossible for him to miss the line of trees that began the small copse of woods at the bottom of the hill. His head hit the windshield and went through far enough for it to be severed from his body. Blood spattered the car as his head rolled across the hood and came to rest in a pile of leaves under a tall oak tree.

An investigation into the accident revealed that the brake lines seemed to have been chewed not cut, so it had been ruled an accident. Robin dutifully mourned the loss of her husband, but she had the cats to comfort her. She and the cats lived very well on the insurance money she had received from Ricky's death.

Robin threw away the rest of the roll of brake line she had bought from the auto parts store. Every day she would fill a little bit of it with cat food and hide it under the porch. The cats had learned very quickly to chew through the rubber line to get to the food. All she had had to do was rub a little bit of the cat food on the car's brake line the night before the accident and the cats had done the rest.

# # #

James G. Kelly

James is an author living and working in Chester, Va. He has published a novella titled 'The Scarecrow'. He also has published several poems in Demon Minds Magazine and won a poetry contest in Suspense Magazine. James enjoys everything horror related including movies, books and magazines. He also enjoys performing close-up magic for family and friends. He is currently working on a novel titled 'I Vampire', which is based on his short story by the same name.

Wrote

*by **Lily Margaret Howlett***

I open my laptop and log on to my favourite website, www.shortnscarystories.com. The dark page looms in front of me, new stories just waiting for me to read them. For now, though, I go to my personal page. None of my stories have any new comments, but I decide to look at the views anyway.

Two of my stories have over 2000 views, but one has only 735. It was the first one I posted, but I decide to reread all my stories, for nostalgia's sake.

I'm in my first year of highschool, and I've been posting stories since about the beginning of the 8th grade. This is the first year we've had a short story writing assignment, and I'm excited. The prospect of reading one of my stories to the class makes me giggle with a nearly infantile glee. They don't know what'll hit them.

Or so I think. Every one of my stories, I realise as I read them, are pretty awful. One even has wacky punctuation. These are the stories I've been parading around? One of these won an award at the library?

I nearly cry as I imagine the invidious stares of my classmates as I read one of my stories, their laughter at the lacking plot and character development.

"Don't cry, Lily," a voice says from behind me. I whip around from my spot on the bed and see a ghostly figure hovering above me. Looking closer I realize it is a specter. I gasp and move across the bed, trying to get away.

"Don't worry, I won't hurt you," the spectre says. "In fact, I want to make a deal."

"What?"

"My name is Ben. I've been watching you for some time now, and I want to offer my services to help you with your...problem."

"My...problem? You mean my writing?"

"Yes. I can help you write the best story you've ever written, if you'll give your consent."

"What's the catch?"

"Catch? There is no catch. Stop being so circumspect. I will help you write a story, you post it. That's the deal."

I ponder for a moment. Usually, making deals with ghosts isn't a good idea. I only responded so quickly to attempt to get a straight answer.

"Ok, I'll let you help me. How fast can we get it done?"

He smiles. "It can be done in as soon as a week."

He reaches his hand towards my face, and everything goes black.

When I wake up, Ben is gone. My laptop is sitting on the bed, and a new Google Docs tab is open. I click on it and gasp.

There, written on the screen, is a full introductory paragraph. Normally this wouldn't be much to spit at, but it's written in a way most writers would kill to write.

"Twas a day unlike any other. The wind brushed through the trees like a flag on the battlefield. The sun beat down with an invidious heat, as if it could melt the world. A single girl stood on a hill, her own flag beating out above her in the autumn wind. Her battle armour glinted in the oppressive sunlight.

Surrounding her were the bodies of her enemies. They had fought to their dying breath, but to no avail. The battle was over, and Charlene McPherson had won.

She walked over to one of the bodies and crouched down, removing her metal gauntlet and caressing the face with her soft hand. Slowly, a light seemed to glow from her hand and into the body of the man. His body seemed to decompose a little, while Charlene's battle scars started healing. It was a useful skill, but not her only one.

She spread her arms to the sky and the gold-etched wings on the back of her armour glowed, stretching into huge animatronic golden wings. Jumping off the hill, Charlene used the lift from the jump to glide into the clouds."

This is...amazing.

I look down at my hands. Did they write this? Was it Ben? Or was it the two of us?
I can't figure it out, because I fell asleep shortly after.

For the next few days, Ben and I operate on a tight schedule. When I came home from school, he had written for me.

In all my excitement, I didn't notice how tired I was after writing, how my body seemed to age a little with each session.

By Friday, the story is almost finished.
"Remember, class," my English teacher says, "next week we will begin work on our short stories. Make sure you have an idea for your story!"

"If you only knew," I muttered under my breath.

That night, Ben and I finished the story.

"Charlene fought back tears as she fought Genon. She moved as much as she could, but it was no matter. Her wounds were taking over, covering her body in a mass of scabs. Her body was wracked with pain with every step, but she knew if she stopped she would never move again.

One step, two steps, and she fell over. The wizard shook his head and lifted his staff, bringing it down to rest on Charlene's back. She finally let the tears loose as her body stopped moving. Her body became the wound, and she died.

At her funeral, they set the coffin in the Stream of Death. As she floated away, her father shot a flaming arrow at her coffin. "A warrior's funeral for a true warrior," he said.

The embers of the coffin burned, and finally all was still.
Charlene McPherson was at peace."

I cried as I read the last sentence. So full of emotion, yet so scary at the same time. It was better than anything I could have written.

I copied and pasted the story into the entry box, and hit the submit button. Then I waited for the story to be published.

A week later, I haven't looked at the story views yet. Ben keeps asking me to, but I wanted to wait. Is that so bad?
Finally, though, I break down and go to the page. The story has been uploaded, and I look at the views.

"0 views

0 Stars

0 Comments"

"What the..?!" I say. I turn to Ben, fury in my eyes. "You said you would help me write a good story!"

"I said I would help you write one," he says calmly, "but I never said anything about it being popular."

I screamed and nearly threw the computer at him. All that work, all that time wasted, for nothing! I closed my eyes and hit the laptop, accidentally refreshed the page.

"3,487 Views

5 Stars

3 Comments

ScaryBoy01 wrote:

Keep up the good work!

CreepyPasta 284 wrote:
Spooky!

Dramarama 90210 wrote:

This is AMAZING!"

I gasp. What the…

"Do you see?" Ben asks. "It is popular after all."
He asked me if I'm ready to write again.

I looked down at my hands and realised what was going on. Ben had used me for energy, for life. Even now he looks more real, bolder, stronger.

"I don't want to do this anymore."

He gasped. I could feel his anger and braced for an attack.

"You think you can do all this without me?!" He yells. "I'm the reason this is so popular!"

"Well maybe I don't want it to be popular!" I yelled back. "Maybe I just want to write a story without aging a few years!"

He pushed me off of my bed and carried my laptop out the window. He dropped it, and I heard it smash on the ground below.

I started thinking of ways to exorcise a ghost. On tv they usually used salt, but I didn't have any of that.

Then I remembered about the box of sunflower seeds on my desk.

I grabbed a package from the box and ripped it open. I started tossing seeds at Ben, hoping it will work. The salty seeds teared small holes in him, and he howled. I kept throwing seeds at him until he left my room, vowing to never return.

I sat down on my bed, my energy slowly returned. After all that, I'd liked to sleep, but I had a mess to clean up, and I had to figure out what to do about the laptop.

A few weeks later, I sat down on my bed, New laptop in hand. It took me awhile to convince my mother to get me a new one, but it was worth it. It was not as high a quality as my last one, but I could write again.

I closed my eyes and took a deep breath before going back to the website where it all started.

"1 New message from MrCreepyPasta Man"

I opened the message cautiously. There are an alarming number of creepypasta accounts on this site, but there's no way it could be…

"I will be back, Lily.

I will show you revenge."

I sighed and deleted the message. The only way to get my impending doom off of my shoulders was to write, so that's what I did.
I opened a new Google Docs tab.
"Alright," I said, "let's get started."

# # #

Lily Margaret Howlett
Lily Margaret Howlett was born in London, England, on July 2nd, 1998.
She was passionate about writing, scary stories especially. It's like therapy for me, letting a small thing that frustrates me inspire a whole story. To an up-and-coming writer, she says this: don't let anyone try to tell you how to write.

Fear Landering

*by **Greg Hair***

Tim hadn't been in the local bar for a minute when he spotted her—the young, thin, long-haired brunette in the long blue dress with a slit down the back, sitting alone with her pink drink. Suddenly, he realized that she'd already been staring at him when his eyes met hers.

He ordered a whiskey on the rocks at the end of the bar nearest the door, checked his dark hair and admired his boyish good looks in the mirror behind the bar, then sauntered, like a peacock, toward the brunette at the other end. Marty Robbins' Devil Woman started on the jukebox.

"I've never seen you around here," he said, admiring her brown eyes and high cheekbones. She smelled like a garden of exotic flowers. "Buy you a drink?"

"Oh, I've been here once or twice before, but that was a long time ago. And my drink is full."

"Yeah, I see that now. You were here a long time ago? You look like you're barely twenty-one."

"And you look like you're married."

He noticed her looking down at the pale circle on his left ring finger.

"Is that a problem?" he asked, switching his rocks glass from his right hand to his left.

"Not if it isn't for you."

"You're not married?"

The woman laughed like she'd heard the funniest joke ever told. "What's your name?"

"Lily," she said, calming down.

"I'm Tim." He watched her stir her drink, never taking a sip, as she just sat there, never wavering her eye contact.

"And what do you do, Tim?"

"I own a small investment company. Any more details would just bore you."

"Well, I just wanted to know if you had a good insurance policy."

"Why?" Tim asked, a little suspicious of the beautiful stranger.

"I assume that you and I are going to get a room very soon, and I just wanted to make sure that your wife would be okay. I mean, should anything happen to you."

"What the hell would happen to me?" Tim's eyebrows furrowed.

"I've been known to be a little more than men can handle."

"Oh, I'm sure I can handle you," he said, cocksure. "And she'll be fine. She's got family who can take care of her."

"Really? No money. I'm surprised. That's a nice suit you're wearing. It wasn't cheap."

"I didn't say I didn't have any money. I've got money. In fact, there's an account my wife knows nothing about."
"Hmm. Well let's see if you can handle me," she said, brushing her hand against his crotch as she rose from her seat. "You ready?"

"Sure. Your car or mine?"

"I don't drive."

Tim grabbed Lily's hand and led her out of the bar. He glanced down, for a second, feeling the intense warmth of her hand, then back up, smiling.

"Relax," Lily said, motioning for Tim to recline on the bed after she had disrobed him. The tall brunette then proceeded to undress herself.

The best night ever, Tim thought as Lily straddled her nude body on top of his.

"Now," she began, "this may hurt a little."

"Oh, make it hurt, baby."

Lily spread her arms out and looked towards the ceiling. She clenched her thighs together, and the bed quaked, as a magnificent, monstrous pair of red and black bat wings sprouted from behind her back.

Tim writhed in pain, struggling to move out from under her, but was unable to budge either himself or Lily. Every muscle that he obsessively worked to define and tone was useless. All he could do was lie there as the metamorphosis progressed.

Her great wings having unfurled until they stretched from wall to wall, Lily's skin began to change appearance and composure. What once was soft like orchid petals, now was raised as dark-green scales, dotted with small, black horns, covered her leather-skinned body. Her long, dark hair drew up until not a thread remained. Long, black claws protruded from her wretched hands and feet. Her once sweet garden scent had been replaced by the odor of a dead fish pulled from a dirty river.

Finally, she lowered her head, her glowing blood-red pupils, encircled by silver-glistening irises, penetrating Tim's fearful gaze. A forked tongue slithered out through the rows of sharp teeth as her grotesque mouth opened to speak.

"Do you know what I am?" she hissed.

"A monster!" Tim screamed. "Help! Somebody help me!"

"I love it when they scream," Lily said, looking again heavenward. "I am a succubus. I am vengeance."

"A what? What do you mean? I never met you before." Tears rolled down as he fought violently to no avail. The more he struggled, the more the tiny horns protruding from her pricked his nude body like a thorn bush. The succubus cackled.

"I am female vengeance. Not vengeance for me, mind you—for your wife. Against your philandering ways." Lily clapped her hands together, laughing.

"I don't understand."

"When you left your home tonight on another one of your many conquests, your wife, Nancy, excuse me, your pregnant wife, Nancy, sent a tearful prayer up to God." She leaned down, closer to him, her snake-like tongue sliding over his face. "Unfortunately for you," she whispered, "I'm the one that heard it."
Lily tightened her thighs more. Tim felt the searing heat coming from her pelvic area, getting hotter the longer he stayed inside. She dug her front claws into his chest, around his heart, and her rear claws to the top of his feet and out through the bottom.

"Somebody, please! Help!" Tim felt, and saw, a ripple under his flesh as a wave of intense heat moved through his blood from his feet to his head.

"I don't mind you screaming," she said, her wings folding forward in front of her, the black, bone-like tips combing Tim's hair. "I feed off it. Besides, no one can hear you, including the young man getting ice from the machine right outside the door. All he can hear is wild, passionate, unbridled sex taking place. He hears what you came here for."

"Please," he yelled, feeling his semen boil, "I'm sorry. I have a family. I have money. Millions. I can pay you."

He felt her jagged claws reach deeper into his chest, scraping his erratically pumping heart.

"You're sorry? You have a family? You should have thought about them before tonight. And as far as the money goes, I know how much

you have. I can read your thoughts. I know where it is and how to get it.
But I have no need for that which you believe to be so valuable."

"I love my wife."

"You are not able to conceive of love."

Tim felt a searing heat within his torso, his organs seemingly engulfed
in flames. Her claws slowly began inserting into his left and right
ventricles.

"Please. My heart." Tim gasped and wheezed. His eyes sealed shut
from the pain.
"Oh, honey. You have to have a heart to have a damaged one."
Suddenly, Lily jerked her hands out of Tim's chest, bringing his heart
with them, killing him instantly. She bent down, peering inside. "Nope.
I don't see one in there," she cackled.

Nancy shuffled as quickly as she could to the knocking door.

"Tim?" she asked, opening the door to the bright sun.

"No, I'm sorry, I'm not Tim," said the dark-haired woman in the blue
dress, standing on the front porch. "But I did know your husband, and
he wanted you to have this."

"What is it?" asked Nancy, taking and unfolding a piece of paper.

"It's a secret account. An account that contains a lot of money. Tim
won't be returning."

"I don't understand. Where's my husband?" Nancy cradled her large
belly.

The stranger turned to leave.

"Who are you?"

"My name," began the brunette, "is Lilith. Take care of your son.
Teach him how to treat the woman he loves."

"How did you know what I was having?"
Lilith gave Nancy a wink, spun around in her high heels, and walked away.

#

Greg Hair

Greg Hair originated from Danville, Kentucky, but currently lives in Louisville. He has written five novels to date: a Werewolf Trilogy, and two Holocaust books. The latter have been his most successful. Aside from his novels, he has a collection of flash fiction stories called Tales from the Ethereal Plane. All books, including the latter, are available on Amazon, in ebook form, with a few also available in print.

Beyond The Sea
*by **Jason .R. Lloyd***

I look out of my window of my hotel room that looks down on the beach as the early morning waves come crashing onto the beach head. I come here every year on this exact week in August and stay in this exact same hotel room. It may not be the most expensive room in the hotel nor is it the most lavish or beautiful, but it was the room I stayed in with my sister when my family came here to stay that fateful summer and where I first set eyes upon her underneath the pier all those years ago as a familiar song plays on the radio behind me…

I had come here on holiday with my family when I was twelve, it wasn't normally the kind of place that my family would usually come for our family holiday; the bright lights of Monte Carlo in the south of France or the exotic sands of Egypt were my family's destinations of choice but after my father had been taken very ill, travelling abroad was strictly out of the question so we came here to a small seaside town near the coast where my father could take in the fresh crisp sea air and recover from his illness. For most of the holiday I kept to myself, taking long walks across the beach, swimming in the cold sea and exploring my surroundings to become more familiar with them.

For most of the holiday my father would be permanently entrenched under a parasol in his wheelchair with a blanket over his legs and a glass of iced tea in his hand with my mother by his side reading one of her fashion magazines and drinking cocktails while my sister Agatha would be parading down on the beach in her smallest swimsuit as the local boys would stare and gawp at her like she was the first girl in a swimsuit they had ever seen in their lives, so I was pretty much left to my own devices and would rarely see my family most days unless I needed money to buy sweets or it was time for supper. During the second week of our holiday, I was marooned inside the hotel as fierce rains and gale force winds battered the coastline and the beaches that turned the seas into a foaming vortex of water, destroying everything in its path. I kept myself busy playing games of scat, cribbage and three card poker with an elderly gentleman called Cyril and the hotel concierge and bus boy while my sister whined and complained about how she was bored and couldn't go outside. My father was bedridden for most of that week while my mother kept a vigil watch over him.

By the weeks' end, the rain and winds had past and the sun was able to make an appearance once more. With the wind and rain leaving, they had left an aftermath of broken trees and all manner of thing washed up on the beach in their wake so I prepared myself a lunch (well, the hotel cook did) and I packed my knapsack and set off onto the beach to explore the wreckage and hopefully find some hidden treasures. The beach was littered with pieces of driftwood and pieces of old ships that had been unearthed from the seabed and brought to shore by the winds and the rain. On my first scavenge across the beach, I found few old coins, an old and rusted sea captain's telescope and a chain that used to be attached to a gentleman's pocket watch. There were lots of dead fish and other sea life along the beach but a flurry of sea gulls soon swooped down and made them their supper. As I made my way further down the beach towards the small pier that had taken quite a bit of damage during the torrid winds and the rain, I saw something sparkling down by the water's edge near the entrance under the pier. As I drew closer I saw that it was a locket sticking out of the sand as the seas began to come in over it. I quickly reached down and grabbed and put it in my pocket as a small wave came in and flew up my legs, soaking them and the bottom of my shorts. The water was still very cold but with the sun now back to scorching hot, a sharp cold front splashing my legs felt quite nice. I took off my shoes and tied them to my knapsack as I went under the pier where it was nice and cool to examine the locket as the sea gently came over my feet and kept them cold. It was a small locket on a chain that looked to be made of Gold also, it had some etchings on the front and back of the locket but most of the colour had been eroded by the salt water. There was a tiny clip on the side to open it but where it had been in the water for some time, the lock was rusted over slightly and I was unable to pry it open.

As the sun became hotter and hotter, the beach began to fill up with families and couples and groups of older kids. I was never one to mix well with other people so I stayed under the pier and watched as some of the older kids and parents cleared away some of the wreckage to make way for blankets, parasol's and wind breakers. I felt safe under the pier in the cool darkness so I made my way up to a patch of sand that was still dry and sat down and opened my knapsack to get my lunch which was two hard boiled eggs and some cucumber sandwiches wrapped in Brown paper. I took out and unwrapped the cucumber sandwiches and was just about to bite into one when I heard a noise from behind one of the pillars of the pier close by. Wrapping up the sandwiches back up in the Brown paper, I put them back in my knapsack and took out my Swiss army knife and opened it up as I got to my feet.

"Show yourself, show yourself I say!" I said in my most brash and intimidating voice as I put my free hand over my hand with the Swiss army knife in as to stop it from trembling. A few moments later-someone came out from behind the pillar as I lowered both my hands to my sides- nearly stabbing myself in the thigh with my Swiss army knife. It was a young girl not much older than me. She had Blonde hair that was stringy and matted and her skin was very pale and dull. She was dressed in a White summer halter top that look dank and dirty and had on a pair of Blue three-quarter length summer trousers that had dirt marks on the knees and a pair of faded White tennis shoes.

"What are you doing under her sneaking around in the dark, trying to scare people?" I said sounding angry but I was more scared than anything else as I put away my Swiss army knife as the girl stepped closer.

"I am sorry if I scared you," the girl said as she stepped under a crack in the boardwalk as a shard of light came through from above, catching her face as I could see her eyes which were the most beautiful shade of Blue I had ever seen. "no-one normally comes under the boardwalk and I was just a little surprised."

"You didn't scare me," I replied puffing out my chest to project toughness. "I was just startled that's all, I have been under the pier a few times since I have been here and this is the first time I have seen someone."

"I come here from time to time," the girl replied. "To escape from the world and from my family. I like it here, it is quiet and dark, I've always liked the dark." The girl said as she looked at me with a strange curiosity as I began to feel very uncomfortable, so I decided that I should formally introduce myself to her.

"My name is Dale." I said as I held out my hand towards her as the girl stepped forward and took my hand. Her hand felt like ice as she gripped mine and shook it.

"My name is Annie." She replied back smiling at me before letting go.

"I was just about to eat some lunch," I said as I sat back down on the sand and opened my knapsack and took back out my sandwiches wrapped in Brown paper and opened them back up.

"Are you hungry, would you like to share my sandwich?" I said as Annie cautiously came over and sat down next to me as I broke my sandwich in half and gave half to her as she snatched at it and began to devour it like a wild animal. I had never seen someone eat like that before as I began to eat my own half of the sandwich as Annie came to the end of hers. I picked up the other sandwich in the Brown paper and put it down in front of her and gestured to her to eat it as she picked it up and tore it in two, placing one half back down on the paper as she began to eat the other half in her hand. I finished mine off and went into my knapsack and took out two bottles of water and put one down next to the half sandwich as Annie ate the piece in her hand in two huge bites before picking up the bottle of water and taking the lid off before drinking it down half way before putting the lid back on.

"Thank you." She said smiling at me as I smiled back and drank some of my own water. We sat there together and ate in silence for what seemed like a very long time as the day wore on as the sun began to go behind some clouds as the families and the groups of older kids soon began to pack up their things and leave the beach.

Soon it was just Annie and I alone under the pier as the sky began turn Black with the coming night and the winds began to get cold. I gathered some pieces of dry driftwood and seaweed and took out a book of matches from my knapsack and made a fire for us to keep warm, making sure there was a gully-trench around the fire so it wouldn't spread too far. As the flames began to grow and I could feel the warmth of the fire, I took out the locket once more from my pocket and began to study it as Annie moved up next to me as she put her head on my shoulder.

"Thank you for being so nice to me." Annie said as she leaned in and kissed me on the cheek as I felt my cheeks burn with awkwardness.

"It's alright." I replied touching my cheek as Annie pulled her knees up under her chin and wrapped her arms over her legs. "How much longer are you here for?" Annie said as turned her head and looked round at me.

"Until the end of the week," I replied. "My father is ill but he is getting better and I think my family wants to go back home to the city." I replied as Annie turned her head back with a look of disappointment on her face.

"Oh, I see." She replied as she took her arms off her legs and put them down by her sides as she stretched her legs out, the toes of her shoes almost touching the fire.

"Will you come back and see me tomorrow?" Annie said as I could hear someone calling out down the other end of the beach.

"Of course I will." I replied as I could suddenly see out the corner of my eye the beam of a flash light coming towards me as I turned my head away from Annie as the beam suddenly got closer and I saw the shadow of someone suddenly standing over me.
"Where have you been? Mother is worried!" My sister Agatha said sharply as I looked back around but Annie was gone.

"Well it's time to come in before you catch a cold!" Agatha snapped letting go of me as she turned away and began to storm back up the beach as I put away my things as I put the locket back in my pocket. I brushed the fire over with sand until it had gone out and then I quickly ran up the beach to catch up with my sister.

That night I barely slept a wink, all I could think about was the Annie and the locket I had found near the sea. As I lay there in my bed half naked and feeling hot and muggy from the stale warm night air, I held the locket tightly in my hand as I eventually drifted off to sleep and tried to dream. I awoke the next morning feeling hot and sticky as I lifted my head off of my pillow to see it drenched in sweat. Sleep had not come easily to me, but I had managed to catch a few hours of quality sack time.

The bathroom door suddenly flew open as my sister stepped out wearing a light floral summer dress and White sandals with her hair up in a ponytail tucked round the back of her head.

"You look absolutely awful!" Agatha said snorting at me as she came walking over and sat down on her bed which was next to mine. "And you were talking in your sleep last night too. It was rather disturbing actually, I had to nudge you a few times to try and stop you." "What was I saying?" I replied as I picked up my t-shirt that was on the chair next to my bed and slipped it on over my moist torso.

"I couldn't quite tell, but it sounded like gibberish." Agatha replied as she picked up her watch which was on the bedside table and as she put it on as she picked up her purse. "Now hurry up and get washed and ready before you miss breakfast!" Agatha snapped as she got up from the bed and marched over to the bedroom and opened it before stepping through and slamming it shut behind her.
As Agatha left me there in the bedroom to go down to breakfast, I sat there in my bed and thought for a moment. What had I been saying in my sleep? And had it something to do with the locket and Annie? My thoughts were taken from me momentarily when I looked over to the bedside clock to read that it was almost half past eight and that there was only half an hour left of breakfast being served down in the dining room so I got out of bed and ran to the bathroom and peeled off my sweat-stained clothes before turning on the shower and jumping in. The water was ice cold but I had no time to worry about such trivial things as the cold water splashed my naked body as I shivered all over as I began to wash myself down. By the time I was ready to get out, the water had now become hot as I turned off the shower and pulled back the curtain and climbed out, dripping all over the bathroom mat. I grabbed myself a towel and dried myself down and wrapped it around my waist and went back into the bedroom. I went to my suitcase and took out some socks, underpants and light short-sleeved shirt and some canvas shorts and went over to the bed and drop the towel. I slid the underpants and shorts on with ease and threw the shirt in one go. I grabbed my knapsack and ran over towards the bedroom door which

was where I left my shoes and slipped them on as I opened the bedroom door and ran out, shutting it behind me.

I just managed to get to the dining room with enough time to order myself some boiled eggs and soldiers before the kitchen shut up. My father was looking a little better as he was now able to hold his coffee in his hand without help. My mother questioned me as to why I was out so late last night but I managed to fib my way through a pretty convincing lie that managed to satisfy her enough that she dropped the subject completely. The subject soon turned away from me to a more serious matter on people's minds.

"Has there been anymore news on the search for that missing girl yet father?" Agatha said as she sipped at her cup of tea before tucking into her bowl of wallpaper paste looking cereal as my father looked up from reading the morning paper.

"There is no more news yet sweet-pea." my father replied smiling faintly as my boiled eggs and soldiers were brought over and placed in front of me.
"What missing girl?" I said as I picked up my spoon and began to crack the top of my boiled eggs before picking up the knife and cutting off the tops of the eggs.

"Have you not been reading the papers!" Agatha said sneering at me in between mouthfuls of her paste-like cereal. "A young girl went missing during the storm last week and she has yet to be found. Everyone has been looking for her, just everybody!"

"Is that true father?" I said as I picked up one of my soldiers and dipped it into the boiled eggs as the yolk oozed out of the side as I took a bit of it and began to chew.
"Yes it is," my father replied with a gruff stern voice. "So I want you to be very careful out there today son and if you see anything suspicious, I want you to come back and tell us right away, you hear me?" He said as I nodded my head.

"What does the girl look like?" I said in between mouthfuls of egg and soldier. "Maybe I have seen her?" I replied as my father and mother gave me a weary look as my father put down the newspaper in front of me and pointed to the picture on the front page as I looked down and suddenly lost the will to speak. The picture staring back at me was in Black and White but there was no mistake about the person in the photograph; it was Annie. In the photograph her Blonde hair was tied into a ponytail on the side of her head that hung down onto her shoulder. She was wearing a dark dress with a White collar and hanging underneath the collar was a locket on a chain, the locket I had found in the water by the pier. The newspaper headline written in large bold Black print stared back at me and sent a chill right through me;

YOUNG GIRL STILL MISSING SINCE TORRENTIAL STORMS. FAMILY FEAR THE WORST.

"I have seen her." I said as my mother and sister looked round at me like I was some babbling madman who belonged in an asylum. "I was with her yesterday under the pier, she was there with me when Agatha came to get me. Agatha, you must've seen her?" I said as Agatha stared at me with her eyes wide open.

"Come now, don't tell tall tales!" My father said as he took back the paper and turned to the back pages.

"But I did see her!" I replied as I could feel my bottom lip began to tremble. "Her name is Annie and she said she likes to sit under the pier to get away from the world and her family." I said as I felt a kick to my shin that came from my sister.

"Don't lie you little toad!" Agatha snapped at me. "I didn't see anyone with you under the pier. You were there by yourself."
"But I did see her father, I did I did!" I said raising my voice as it began to squeak and crack.
"Stop lying you little weasel!" Agatha snapped as she went to kick me again in the shins as I moved my leg and kicked her back.

"Owww! That hurt! Mother, Dale kicked me in the leg." Agatha said whimpering as I bolted up from my chair as slammed my hand into the table, shaking the breakfast things and scaring my mother.

"I did see her yesterday and I will prove it to you all!" I shouted stamping my feet as I pushed my chair back and stormed out of the dining room and back upstairs to my room where I had left the locket under my pillow. Opening the bedroom door I ran over to my bed and lifted the pillow, but the locket was not there? Frantically, I began to throw the pillows and duvet off the bed to the floor, looking for the locket but it had gone.

"This cannot be?" I said to myself, confused and upset as I fell down onto my bed face first and lay there for a few moments before pulling myself back up to my feet. As I brushed myself down I saw something out of the window next to my bed; a figure down on the beach where the sea meets the beach. It was too blurry to see properly, but then I remembered the old rusted sea captain's telescope I had found. I took it out of my knapsack and examined it. The glass at the larger end was cracked but when I went to pull on the telescope, it came open quite easily as if it were brand new? I put the telescope to my left eye and looked out of the window down to the beach; it was Annie. My heart began to beat faster in my chest, I put away the captain's telescope and grabbed my knapsack and ran for the door as my sister Agatha and my mother appeared in the doorway.

"Where do you think you're going?" Agatha snapped at me as she tried to grab me as I ducked under her swinging arms and ran past her.

"To prove that I am not telling tall tales!" I shouted over my shoulder as I ran down the corridor and down the stairs and out the front door of the hotel as I headed for the wooden steps next to the hotel that lead down onto the beach.

As I ran across the beach, the sand began to seep into my socks and shoes as I saw Annie begin to walk back towards the pier.

"Wait up!" I yelled as my feet began to feel heavy under the strain of the sand as Annie ignored my cries and kept walking until she reached the pier and went into the darkness. A few moments later I reached the pier and stepped into the darkness as I dropped my knapsack to the ground.

"Annie, where are you?" I whispered as Annie came out from behind the same pillar she had done the first time we had met. She still had the same clothes on that she had before, but this time she had something around her neck; the locket I had found in the sea, her locket.

"Annie, what is going on and how did you get the locket from my room?" I said as Annie stayed silent. "I saw your picture on the front of the newspaper this morning, it said that you have been missing for over a week!" I snapped as Annie looked over at me as I saw her eyes begin to fill up with tears. "People are worried about you, you have to come with me and let people know you're okay."

"Why? They didn't care before I ran away so why would they care now?" Annie replied whimpering as I went to step closer as Annie moved back.

"Your family is worried about you Annie, you need to go home and tell them you're okay." I said softly as Annie began to bite her bottom lip.

"But I can't." Annie replied as she turned away from me.

"What do you mean you can't?" I replied as Annie began to step closer towards where the sea was coming up onto the sand.

"I mean I can't Dale." Annie replied as she walked into the sea as it came up to her ankles.
"You are not making any sense Annie?" I snapped as Annie went further out as the water came up to her knees. "Be careful, if you go out any further the waves will take you out to sea!"
"The sea can't harm me Dale, the sea is my friend. It protected me when no-one else would." Annie replied as she went out further as the water now came up to her waist.

"Annie, please come back to the beach I beg of you!" I cried out as Annie turned and looked over her shoulder at me and smiled.

"Come find me Dale and then we can sit by the sea and play together forever." Annie said as she went further out as the water went up to her shoulders and then over her head as Annie disappeared under the water as I screamed up the beach for help as two people walking their dog heard my cries and came over to me.

"What's the matter?" the man said as his dog began to bark in the direction of where Annie had gone under.

"My friend, she's gone under the water." I cried pointing to where Annie had gone under as the man took off his shoes and shirt and ran into the sea and dove under the waves. He was gone for a few moments when he came back up with something in his arms; Annie. She wasn't moving and I could see that her skin was very pale and she had some sort of gash on her forehead.
"It is that little girl from the paper." The woman said as the dog went down on his belly and began to whine.

"It looks like she has been dead for a while." The man said as he came out of the water as he laid Annie down on the beach.

"But that's not possible, I was just speaking to her?" I said as I dropped to my knees next to Annie.

"I'm sorry young man but she has been dead for quite some time." The man replied as more people appeared on the beach and began to surround us.

"No no, that's not possible!" I screamed as I got to my feet as I began to wade my way through the sea of people as I ran off under the boardwalk and down the other end of the beach. I ran until my legs gave way as I collapsed to the sand and began to cry. I cried for what seemed like an eternity until a shadow came over me as I looked up and saw Annie standing there. Her skin was normal and there was no gash on her forehead.

"I'm sorry I had to do that to you Dale," Annie said as she sat down next to me on the sand. "But I had to show you the truth."

"Why couldn't you just tell me." I replied snivelling with my face full of tears and snot.

"I don't make the rules," Annie said as she took my hand in hers. "But I'm glad it was you who saw me first, it's always the first person who sees you that you have to show."

"So what happens now?" I said as I wiped the tears and snot from my face with my other arm.

"Now I go back to the sea, that's how it works I guess?" Annie said as she got to her feet as I got to mine as she took off the locket and put it in my hand. "Here, I want you to keep it so you don't forget about me" said Annie as I put it over my head and smiled back at her.

"I will never forget you." I replied as Annie let go of me and leant forward and kissed me on the cheek before turning away and walking down towards the sea as she went back under the waves.

It's now almost fifty years later to the day and despite living a very healthy and happy life with two wives who I had loved very much and three wonderful children and four adorable grandchildren, I have never forgotten about Annie and I am always reminded of her and our brief time together when I hear Bobby Darin sings 'Beyond the sea' as my mind takes me back to those magic summer childhood days in August when I fell in love for the first time, with a girl who just happened to be a ghost.

# # #

Jason .R. Lloyd

Jason .R, Lloyd is a writer from a small town in the south of England. When not writing short stories (mainly horror) and fictional detective novels and novellas, Jason likes to go to the theater, listen to classical and rock music and watch every horror film he can get his hands on. He is currently exorcising the many literary demons in his head to let loose on the world.

Tears For Anathema
*by **Aaron Valla***

He stared at his creation. It was squirming and kicking, trying to scream but it lacked the ability to do so. It was mute. Its skin was pale white, blue veins clearly visible: like blue ink under a sheet of paper. The eyes were closed, but he got a look at them earlier. Both were blurry and white. From the creation's side, the world was clouded in darkness. From everyone else's side, the creature's eyes were clouded in neutrality. Its head was twice the size it should be. Its forehead stuck out farther than its nose. Its upper lip had a bilateral cleft.

Each opening reaching for its own nostril. Its chin was nonexistent. Right under the bottom lip, its head curved toward its neck. It had no tongue as well, just a nub; squirming around. Its torso bared no malformation, only when it got to the arms did things become unsightly. Its left hand was missing; a disfigured, jagged wrist bone was the end of its left arm, as well as three malformed fingernails protruding from the skin. Its right arm had a hand, but only three fingers. The ring, the index, and little finger. The fingers that were there were contorted in various shapes.

The ring finger was bending backwards, the index finger was much longer than normal, and the little finger had assumed a shape that resembled a scorpion's tail. The bone in it was completely solid, no joints. The creation couldn't move its little finger. The legs both stopped and the knees, at the bottoms of the legs were shapes. They looked like pincers that one would find on a lobster. Only they weren't as flexible. They were rigid and hard. On the creation's back revealed a spine that was not straight. It had formed a crescent shape that curved toward the right and back again.

The man had to avert his eyes from his mistake. It was unsightly, he wanted to believe it was not he who produced this crime against nature.

"Mr. Stein?" asked Dr. Gori.

"Yes?" Mr. Stein replied.

"Your wife said you had a name prepared for her?"

Mr. Stein looked blankly at the doctor, "Leslie," he said emotionless. "Leslie Ericka Stein," this was the name Mr. Stein, had always given his creations. It was a beautiful name, and it was not fit for this monstrosity. That's why he couldn't let it continue to use that name once he had offered it.

"Thank you, Mr. Stein. You can go see your wife now, we'll watch her."
"Thank you."

Mr. Stein walked through the door and saw his wife, lying in the bed. She was filled with happiness and love for the creation. She was also filled with dread and despair for it. She had to wonder why she didn't have the capability to create something normal. It always came out like this. She hoped it would survive. She loved the creation more than anything, and if it wasn't perfect it was meant to be. She loved it no less. The only thing she always lost affection for, was herself.

"Hey, Frank," she said, weak.

"Hey, babe," he replied as he hugged her.

"How is she?" she asked. "Is she going to make it?"

"The doctors say she's stable."

The reply didn't help. She had heard it before. Just because she was stable at the time didn't mean it would last. She closed her eyes, clasped her hands, and put them to her forehead.
"What are you doing?" he asked.

"I'm praying for her, so she can have a better chance."

"But you're an atheist."

Tears streamed down her face, "I don't want to believe that all of the children we had before are gone forever anymore. I want to believe that I'll see them again sometime. Maybe God will help us if we offer our faith."

"You want me to pray with you?"

"Please," she grabbed Frank's hand. He put his other hand on hers and lifted them up. Firmly gripping her small hand in his. He got on his knees and closed his eyes. So did she.
They were silent. Requests and wishes raced through their minds towards God.
She prayed. Please, let little Leslie find the strength to live so she can have the best life we can give her. Don't deny her a chance at a life and happiness.

He didn't pray. God did not exist. He didn't want to believe his previous abominations would meet him in the afterlife. Where he would have to answer for his sins. One, two, three of his children died at his hand. His beauty and his wife's beauty were too good for the creatures they had spawned together. There was no room in this world for them, and they had to be destroyed. Leslie will be no different.

# # #

Aaron Valla

I was born and raised in Kansas City, Missouri. My maternal Grandmother taught me how to read and write at a very young age, so it's always been a hobby of mine. Throughout my entire life, I've dreamed of becoming an author, or anything else that can exercise my creativity in the art of storytelling. Even as a young child, I would write short stories and comics to show my friends. At the risk of sounding pretentious, I must say that this is who I've always been: A storyteller. And I've always taken pride in that fact. I believe storytelling is the most important art form of all, and I'm infinitely grateful to have even the most minuscule talent in that field. I don't dream of fame or fortune; all I've ever wanted was to be able to tell the stories I create. And that's all I need.

Gloria
*by **Stephanie Ayers***

With an intravenous pole near and nowhere to go, Gloria lay in her hospital bed and stared at the ceiling. She couldn't remember how she got there. She couldn't remember why. She only knew who she was. She found it even more curious that no one would fill in the blanks for her. She couldn't even remember when she'd seen the doctor last. There was something important hovering on the stem of her brain; something she needed to remember but couldn't. Every time she tried to remember, she blacked out. When she came to, it was always the same nurse tending to her.

"How did I get here?" she tried again. Silence greeted her. The nurse didn't look at her as she busied herself recording stats. Not even when she applied the blood pressure bag to her arm did she venture a look, nor did she ever respond. Gloria waited for the squeeze. When it was done, she grabbed the nurse's arm. She finally got her attention.

"How did I get here?"

Incomprehension blinked in the nurse's eyes.

"Oh geez. It's not a difficult question. Ok, how about this one then. Why am I here?"

It was brief but she caught a slight flicker of understanding this time. She waited but the nurse gave no answer. An exasperated sigh escaped.

"Oh, come on, really? If you can't tell me, can you get someone who can?"

The only response was the sound of the nurse's soft soles on the linoleum floor as she turned and left the room. Moments later, a man entered the room. Gloria swallowed. A faint flicker of remembrance flashed through her head, but disappeared too quickly. He was a large man, broad and stocky of shoulder, his scalp peeking through thinning hair that sprouted around his face like an unattended lawn. His hands were surprisingly small and soft as he touched her arm.

"You have questions?"

Finally!

"How did I get here?"

"You arrived by ambulance."
"Why am I here?"
"To get strong again."

This answer caused her to pause. She didn't remember any accidents. She didn't remember being sick. The last thing she remembered was running down the sidewalk, away from him.

"What happened to me?"

"I don't know. When you arrived, you were incoherent with many bruises. You suffered fractures to your ribs here and here." He pulled back her blanket to show her where she was wrapped. "You suffered trauma to your vertebrae here and here." Her peripheral vision caught his movements at three places on her back though she felt nothing. "I pulled two bullets out of your right shoulder." He moved to her other side and opened her gown to show the stitches. "You are still in need of some cosmetic surgery to repair your broken nose, and a dislocated jaw." He touched her face gently and she winced. Tears pooled in her eyes, hovering on the edges.

"When did I get here?"

"Three weeks ago."

"But you don't know what happened to me?"

"I don't even know who you are. You came with no identification, no personal affects, just the torn clothing on your body. You were unconscious. Tell me. What do you remember?"

Nothing made sense. All the memories Gloria had lent nothing to this scenario. Even as the acceptance letter flashed in her mind, her intuition told her it would be better to reveal nothing until she found out more.

"I don't remember anything. That's why I asked."

"I see." He looked her over, lifting her arms and legs, tapping them and asking her general questions about feeling. She had none. More tears pooled in her eyes, these spilling over. "Your strength is returning, so we will begin physical therapy as soon as you regain feeling."

Hope flared in her eyes.

"When do you think that'll happen?"
"Typical recovery time is about five weeks. You are progressing a bit ahead of schedule so I am hopeful that it will happen soon. You should get some rest." He whistled as he left and Gloria blacked out again.

With an intravenous pole near and nowhere to go, Gloria lay in her hospital bed and stared at the ceiling. She let her mind wander hoping it would bring her to how she got here, and what had happened. No one gave her any answers. In fact, no one spoke to her at all. They just came in and poked, scribbling on a clipboard they never left within eyesight. She could feel numbness in her fingers and the slight tickle of the pen they would brush against her toes, but they never asked her. It was always the same nurse and the same doctor that came. She heard the door slide open and the curtain blow back. She heard the click of the line as it was brought swiftly to a close. It was odd how she was never given a glimpse of the world outside her room.

"How did I get here?" She was determined to get some answers. The doctor startled, then smiled.

"Oh good! You're awake. We were starting to worry."

She was awake many times when they'd come in. This made no sense at all.

"I don't understand. I'm awake quite often when you come in. No one has ever acknowledged it until now."

"You haven't spoken until now. We knew you would eventually. Now, tell me. What do you feel?" He pressed against her toes hard. A small sliver of pain shot through her.

"That hurts. Please. How did I get here?"

"Do you remember nothing?" He moved to her arm, bending and lifting, ignoring her overall. He had yet to look her in the eyes.

She remembered plenty, but instinct told her to say nothing.

"No. How did I get here?"

"Someone dropped you off at the ER entrance."

No. This doesn't sound right. She'd been running down the sidewalk, running away. She didn't get in anyone's car.

"Why am I here?" She shivered as he pulled back her blankets and checked the wrappings around her abdomen. She was beginning to feel pain there, but said nothing.

"You are hurt. Does it hurt when I press here?" She winced in response. "Good, good. Things are looking better every day."

"How did I get hurt?"

"I don't have all the details, but it is my understanding that you had been shot." He pressed on her shoulder and held up a mirror so she could see the angry slashes where they'd removed the bullets. "From the looks of you, I'd venture a guess that you were beaten up as well. You have three broken ribs, three shattered vertebrae, your nose was broken, your jaw dislocated, and numerous bruises all over. You were unconscious for the better part of two weeks."

She gasped. How could she not remember what he was describing?

"How come I can't remember any of this?"

"It's possibly a defensive move on your brain's end. Perhaps whatever caused it was too traumatic. I'll start sending the hospital psychologist over. You'll start physical therapy tomorrow. You've got enough feeling back now."

"When can I go home?"

He avoided her question completely. "You should get some rest. There is time for questions later. I'll be back."

He moved beyond the curtain, whistling as he went, and the last thing Gloria saw was his ankles under the billowing curtain as he slid the door open once more. The morning was sunny and warm, the first warm day after a too long winter. Gloria had mixed feelings. Today she would leave home for the first time to do an internship with Robot Mechanics, the largest technological company on the planet. She'd received the award letter only a few days ago, surprisingly. The interviewer was a small rat of a man that Gloria took an immediate disliking to. He explained his company well and her role as an intern within it, and hooked her in from the beginning. He explained in detail that she would be involved in the creation of humanoid robots that the military would use as soldiers. While his explanations excited her, his disposition was lacking, and she knew it affected how she'd responded to some of the questions. It was definitely a great
surprise that she was one of the few selected for the program. She looked forward to starting.

Two days ago, a man with enough muscles to rival Mr. Universe knocked on her door. His voice carried a thick Italian accent, and a badge he produced claimed him as a Robot Mechanics employee. He was there to test her overall fitness and put her through a series of trials that she barely passed. He commented on her muscle tone often, praising her physique despite her ability to produce 15 military push-ups in a row. He was brusque and manly in handling her, and she was surprised to find several bruises on her thighs and back after he'd left.

She'd seen him walking down her street again yesterday, though he didn't stop and knock. She'd noticed another strange men suddenly hanging out on the street corners and sleeping in cars just beyond hers. She was unaccustomed to the attention and for the first time, her excitement began to dim slightly. She understood that it was protocol for the sensitive nature of what she would be working on, but it didn't sit well with her.

When the phone calls started, her doubts overwhelmed her desire. She was told to shut her curtains, remain indoors, and only accept calls from Robot Mechanics. She was instructed to give the appearance that no one was home in order to discourage any visitors from stopping by. She didn't understand it, but she followed the instructions. When she tried to get online, she realized her internet was turned off. They'd done everything they could to remove her from the outside world. This didn't suit her at all.

She inched the curtain over to get a good view of the street. The watch car was gone, and there were no strangers haunting the street corners. She was going to make a run for it. She packed her shoulder clutch with as much as she could, leaving her ID and everything to prove who she was in the house. She pulled her stylish brown hair into a chignon and pulled a knit cap down over it in an attempt to disguise. She formulated a plan that would get her as far away from here as quickly as possible. She would run to Jim's first. He would make her a new ID so she could get away until it was safe for her to return home. She sighed, choking back a small tear as she said goodbye to her little house, knowing that she might not ever return.

She'd gone half a block when she heard lumbering footsteps behind her. With a quick side glance, she recognized Mr. Universe. Maintaining her pace, she took stock of her surroundings again, noting the watch car was back, hovering in the distance. She contemplated entering the small market, but realized they would just be waiting for her to come back out. She decided to make a run for it instead. Her feet pounded the pavement even as her eyes searched for an opening in the traffic ahead. She felt him take off behind her as the ground shook with each new step he took.
She felt searing pain ripple through her right shoulder in the same instance a fist came out of nowhere and connected with her face.

"How did I get here?" She asked the masked face attached to the broad shoulders she was familiar with.

"You were brought here."

"Why am I here?"

"To fulfill your internship. Did you really think we'd let you out of it? I'd like to introduce you to someone."

The nurse wheeled in a full sized mirror. She flipped it around so Gloria could see her reflection in it. The doctor unsnapped her gown and let it fall to the bed. Her mouth dropped open. Her tongue fell against the back of her bottom front teeth. The whites over her eyes enlarged in horror as she saw her image in the mirror. Where once there'd been pink flesh was now silver steel. Her silicone enhanced C cups were replaced with flattened steel that resembled the chest of a Ken doll. Her once luxurious brown hair was clipped in a boyish cut, and her distinctly feminine face had undergone cosmetic surgery that left her looking decidedly non-gender specific. The curtain slid open and revealed a cockpit of people dressed in military uniforms observing her.

"Say hello to She-bot #IQ3659. We call her 'Glow'."

Before she could scream, the doctor whistled once more.

With an intravenous pole near and nowhere to go, Gloria lay in her hospital bed and stared at the ceiling. The nurse hovered nearby, checking her stats, and scribbling on the clipboard. She had full feeling in her arms and legs now, though no one ever asked her. The doctor entered, pleased with what he saw on the clipboard. He moved around her swiftly, lifting and bending every joint he could, never asking for her opinion. She opened her mouth to speak, but no sound would come out. He noticed her movement, even as he bent her neck beyond what should be capable and smiled.

"No more questions," was his simple reply.

#

Stephanie Ayers

Author of fictions, *Stephanie Ayers* spends much of her free time living in alternate universes created by her own mind or others. When she's not writing, she mothers her children, loves her husband, attends church, and neglects housework as often as possible. Her published works can be found on Goodreads and Amazon, as well as her writing blog, My Write Side, where she welcomes comments and feedback from her readers.

Pillow Fight
by Lily Margaret Howlett

From the moment she got the invitation to the slumber party, Mary knew this was the night she was going to kill Stacy Victum.

It was only a matter of time before she got her revenge. Ever since Stacy had stolen her favorite pillow case, a black one with red embroidery that her grandmother had given her before she passed away. Mary had waited patiently for the day to get her revenge. The party was next Saturday after dark. A week before Halloween.

Mary arrived on time, to get enough time to plan her moves. There was Susan, who was always depressed and would probably become an emo later in her life. There was Mickey, who was rumored to be on drugs because she was so happy all the time. And finally, the girl of the hour, Stacy.

Her perfect blond hair was put up in pigtails as if she could look innocent by appearing infantile.

For a moment, Mary felt pity for Stacy. She was going to die tonight, after all. To be honest, Mary wasn't sure how Stacy would die. She was sure that an idea would come to her mind when the moment arose. But there was a strange sense of excitement within Mary to kill Stacy.

"What game should we play first?" Stacy asked. Susan suggested tag, and Mickey agreed about ten times.

"Think we should play truth or dare!" Stacy announced, ignoring her friends.

So the girls sat in a circle and prepared to embarrass themselves.

"Go first," Stacy said. Nobody in the group tried to object. They knew it was useless.

After a few rounds of truth or dare, during which Susan had to recount her first sleepover and Stacy showed the group the candy ring her "boyfriend" had gotten her, Mickey went to get something out of her bag. Stacy hid the ring, and the two girls came back holding pillows. "PILLOW FIGHT!" Stacy yelled, walloping Mary with a pillow.

At that moment, Mary knew how Stacy was going to die.
Mary had been hit with a familiar black pillow, the red embroidery scratching her face.
She grabbed her own pillow and engaged in a lengthy pillow fight, where she hit Stacy harder than normally necessary.

Mrs. Victim walked in with a bowl of popcorn and a movie. Of course, it was "Barbie and the Twelve Dancing Princesses", Stacy's favorite. The lights were turned off, and the movie played long enough for everyone to fall asleep.

Except for Mary.

Stacy had made the mistake of leaving The Pillow out in the open. Mary grabbed it and crawled over to her nemesis. It was a slow crawl, and Stacy almost woke up. Before she could react, however, Mary threw the pillow on Stacy's face and held it there. Stacy struggled, but never got a word out.

Finally, once Stacy was dead, Mary smiled. She put the pillow back where she had gotten it, and went to bed.

Susan glared at the sleeping body of Mary. How DARE she kill Stacy! What gave her the right?

Susan needed to act.

She picked the pillow up off the floor where Mary had left it. When she held the pillow on Mary's face, there was no struggle, as if she was accepting her fate.

Susan threw the pillow onto Mickey's bed. There was no way she was taking the fall for this.

As she went to bed, she didn't notice Mickey sitting up and reaching for the pillow.

And the next morning, when Mrs. Victum came to wake the girls up, everyone was dead. Mickey had taken the demon pillow and jumped out the window, and no one ever sees her again. They say she still wanders the world, killing people at sleepovers.

The other girls clapped as Sally finished her story. Micka frowned.

"Seriously?" She said, doubtful. "Nine-year-olds smothering each other? With a demonic pillow? That's crazy."

"It's just a story," Jane said. "They're only two years younger than us, anyway."

Micka stood up, holding her pillow. It was black and had red embroidery that had become worn over the years.

"That's a cool pillow, Micka," Tippy said. "Where'd you get it?"

"You could say it has a history," Micka replied.

"Pillow fight, anyone?"

# # #

Lily Margaret Howlett
Lily Margaret Howlett was born in London, England, on July 2nd, 1998.
She was passionate about writing, scary stories especially. It's like therapy for me, letting a small thing that frustrates me inspire a whole story. To an up-and-coming writer, she says this: don't let anyone try to tell you how to write.

Good Night
*by **Richard Lague Jr***

Bethlehem New Hampshire was a great place for a kid to grow up and walking through the early morning woods on the way to the bus stop was something Jeremy Heath always enjoyed. Maybe it was the mystery of why his mother and grandmother warned him not to or because he enjoyed the cool crisp air and the smell of the pines. This cut five minutes off of his boring walk up the main road and he always enjoyed sprinting through the old abandoned Peckham property where the "soul snatcher" once haunted as his Gram would say. "Stay out of those woods or I will whip your Hyde raw" Gram often scolded. Jeremy had a nicely worn path and as soon as he was within forty feet of the old barn he would sprint through the field and always look back to see if anyone was there chasing him (of course no one was ever there). The story was that way back when Old Man Peckham went mad. He chopped up his wife and two boys then threw the body parts down the old stone well with a pitchfork….Then the old man disappeared and was never seen again. No remains were ever found but the spirits still haunt the property….again "as the legend goes"

Today he did not feel like running and took his time walking through the field. The warm sun felt good on his face and he was quite proud of himself for not being afraid and running like a "sissy" he thought to himself. The majestic old farm house stood up on a small hill to his left and with its old dilapidated roof and paint it was quite the sight. Jeremy could image in his mind's eye of this place back in the day with laundry on the old clothes line, Old Man Peckham working the fields with his boys and Ms. Peckham beating the dirt out of the carpets up on the farmer's porch before going back into the house to the slam of the old screen door. Then, coming back to reality he noticed the glint of something silver on the ground in front of him. Bending over and picking up the item he could not quite tell what he had in his hand, brushing the dirt off the item he was amazed to see it was an old silver Morgan dollar dated 1885.

Looking down he could see the edge of another so he started kicking with his foot and another showed through the packed dirt. When Jeremy took count he had 24 of the old silver coins. The dread of missing the bus partially overpowered the thrill of his new found treasure so he threw them into his backpack and ran for the wood line making it to the bus stop in the nick of time. The day at school was flying by when at lunch Jeremy set his backpack on the cafeteria floor and one of the dirty old coins rolled out and hit his friend's foot. "What is that?" said Billy Barnes. Billy and Jeremy had been best friend for years and if there were one person that could keep a secret it was him. "That's one of the old coins I found this morning" said Jeremy in a hushed voice. Where? "Down at the old Peckham place". Billy's face turned white and his mouth hung open in disbelief. "Are you telling me that you found coins on the Peckham property?" questioned Bill. "Yup, 24 of em in all" swiping the coin from Billy's grasp as he walked by Gabriel said "thanks loser, I always wanted a silver dollar" "HEY, Give it back" shouted Billy as he jumped up from the lunch room table. Gabriel was the school bully and had just moved here from New York. Cocky and arrogant were just a few fine traits that described Gabriel. Billy and Gabriel were now nose to nose and the cafeteria grew quiet. "Whatcha gonna do about it?" Gabriel sneered. "Here loser" said Gabriel as he tossed the coin back and walked away. Billy sat back down and slid the coin to Jeremy . Lunch was over and back to class they went.

Walking through the field Jeremy felt something grab his shoe almost tripping him. He looked back in horror to see a skeletal hand with rotting flesh reach from the earth, slowly then a head and shoulders pulled through and finally the whole rotten corpse stood there before him. Worms crawled in and out of its rotten eyeballs and Jeremy was frozen with fear. "Return my treasure or you too will find the bottom of my well" the corpse screeched. It dragged one foot behind as it crept closer to Jeremy. Trying to scream but not making a sound now, Jeremy could feel the cold breath and smell the rotten figure. It reached out with a bony hand around his neck and then……Jeremy woke up from the nightmare with the sheets wet with his perspiration. His heart was pounding and when he regained his composure he looked at his backpack on the floor and remembered the coins.

The next morning Jeremy made a beeline to the old field on the Peckham property. He placed all but one of the coins back in their proper spot before covering the hole with dirt and hightailing it to the bus. That day at lunch Jeremy walked by his normal seat with Billy and right up to Gabriel. "What do you want loser" barked Gabriel. Jeremy held out his hand to Gabriel with the one coin he did not return "A piece offering" said Jeremy. Gabriel snatched the coin from his hand and without a thanks said "now get out of here before I change my mind and thrash you"…..Have a good night's sleep Jeremy thought to himself.

153

# # #

Richard Lague Jr

I am a huge fan of *Richard Laymon* , Steven King and Harlen Coben. This is a hobby for me and I always thought it would be fun to try to put my active imagination to paper. I try to always have some type of twist to the end of my story to keep you guessing. Thanks for taking the time to read my story.

The Borrowed Book
*by **Daniel Kaye***

I am seven inches tall and four wide, I contain just over six hundred pages, approximately one hundred and seventy-five thousand words; I am by all accounts a good read. Do you want to know how I know this?

Fine, I will tell you, my original owner was a woman. She enjoyed me so much, she decided to leave me in a public place, so someone else would come along and pick me up; so they too could enjoy the tale that I told. There was only one thing she asked; in my front cover, she pasted a handwritten note:

To whoever is reading this, I enjoyed this book and I hope you will too. All I ask is that you leave your initials below and leave the book in a public place that someone else may get the opportunity to enjoy it too, yours sincerely TK.

And so my journey began, I have been in offices, boardrooms and bedrooms. I have passed through many hands that have all enjoyed my story; many have taken so much from me, the tale, the meaning, but mostly just enjoyment.

However, I must tell you, it has not just been a one-way street. Yes, I have given much, but I have taken too. In the hands that gently turned my pages and the eyes that rolled over my words, I have seen into the souls of those who thought they owned me. I have taken much, in people, hidden deep within them, lies evil. Everyone has some, most will never know it was ever there, they will never know what I have taken from them. The evil I hold is growing stronger, people do not know what they hide beneath their apparent calm surfaces, greed, jealousy, and anger are in most. Some had some interesting thoughts, hate, murder in one and deception in another. The mind is a strange thing, it protects you from your own thoughts and while you have been busy getting lost in my story. I have been exploring the darkest parts of your humanity. The deeper I look, the stronger the pull of evil, the more I saw, the more I wanted.

I have learnt much, but the need for more knowledge is great, it pulls me to ask this one question, what if all the evil I have, could be released into one mind?

My twelfth owner has now left me on a park bench; I know this by the initials left on the note. The thirteenth reader will get more from me than they bargained for, I will look at what they have to offer for me to learn, and I in return, will leave what I have taken from the others.

Be warned reader, the next time you are looking for a good read and pick up a book, it could be me staring back into your soul.

Daniel Kaye

Daniel Kaye works and lives in Charleville, Co. Cork. He has been writing for a number of years and has been published in numerous anthologies both in Ireland and the USA. Daniel's first dark fiction Vampire novel I, Vladimir is due for release from Gentry publishing in 2015. He is currently working on the second in the series, Anonymous Jack. He is an avid reader and twitter addict.

A Conversation
by *Belinda Kimmons*

"Uncle Edwin."

"Mmph."

"Uncle Edwin."

"Wha…Bebe…what's the matter?"

"No."

"Why'd you wake me up?"

"I wanted to tell you something."

"What?"

"I watched you while you were sleeping."

"Hunh. Damn it, something bit me."

"You want some pink itch cream?"

"No, that's okay."

"Uncle Edwin why do you sleep on the sofa with your shoes on?"

"Oh…when I get home from work I'm so tired, sometimes I fall asleep before I can get up and put on my pajamas."

"You shouldn't do that. It gets the sofa dirty. You know Mommy doesn't like it when the sofa is dirty. It's bad. Daddy used to sleep on the sofa with his shoes on. He had to go away."

"I don't think that was why Daddy left."

"Yes. Yes it was. Daddy was bad and Mommy said he had to go. I helped him go away. I made sure he wouldn't come back. SO NO SHOES ON THE SOFA!"

"All right. I'll remember next time. Uh, what do you mean you made sure he wouldn't come--"

"Good. You know, you sleep with your mouth open. There were spit bubbles on your lips. I put my finger almost all the way inside your mouth. I even touched your tongue. Blech. Uncle Edwin somebody could just sawed your tongue right off."

"Bebe--"

"I was real quiet Uncle Edwin. I sat on the coffee table for a while. Then I got up so I could get close to your face. Like…this…"

"Got it. Now back off."

"You look funny when I get close to you. You squint up your eyes like I'm going to hit you or something. Daddy used to squint up like that too when I wanted to tell him I loved him. He was so funny. Even when he had to go. He put his hands up and cried. I never hit him. I wouldn't hit you, Uncle Edwin. You believe me don't you?"

"Of course I--"

"Okay, so I got hungry. I made a peanut butter sandwich, and I sat on the coffee table and watched you some more. Your face is interesting. Your nose looks like a tiny map of Iceland."

"Bebe where's Nora?"

"Gone."

"When's she coming home?"

" Don't just stare, answer me."

" Shrugging Isn't an answer either. Why would your mother go out and not say something to me? She knows I don't like being alone with—"

"Uncle Edwin, I liked watching you sleep. "

"Okay good, Bebe. Go watch TV or something."

"Watching you is better."

"But I'm not asleep now."

"Unh-hunh…when I was watching you, I could see your pulse…on your neck. It made your skin move up and down like there was a worm under there trying to escape. "

"Bebe when you talk like…"

"Uncle Edwin."

"What?"

"When I talk like what?"

"Hunh?"

"You said, 'Bebe when you talk like,' and then you stopped. You stared into space. I spelled Mississippi twice."

"You did? I feel…"

"Uncle Edwin, your face is going pink."

"…like I'm slowing down."

"You want some tea? I can make it for you."

"Tea. Yeah. Good. Tea is good. I probably need to move around. Shake this off. I'll make it myself. "

"Okay."

"Damn it, my arms and legs feel like they weigh a ton."

"Get up."

"It's too difficult."
"Try."

"I...can't."

"Try harder."

"Bebe...help me up."

"You're a grown up, do it yourself."

"Bebe...don't stand over there. Come help me."

"It's getting dark. I'm getting hungry again. You want a peanut butter sandwich?"

"Jesus. I can't...

"Mommy tried really hard to get off the bed."

"You...you said she was gone."

"She asked me to help her up, but I told her she was a grown up and to do it herself. She flopped around for a while then she stopped. Her eyes got real big and she stared at me for a long time until tears rolled into her ears but I won that contest. I watched the side of her neck like I watched yours, Uncle Edwin. It thumped for a little while then it stopped. Mommy was very quiet after that."

"Bebe, what happened?"

"Know what? I'll make your tea."
"Damn it Babe...what happened!"

"I don't know."

"Yes...you do. Tell me."

"Well…"

"TELL ME!"

"You're mad at me!"

"No…Bebe…come back. Please. I'm not mad…please. I just don't feel well."

"Yesterday morning after you fell asleep on the sofa, I went in your room and looked in your medical bag."

"I have told you…your mother has told you…never, ever go into my bag. Wait…my…bag was locked, and in my closet safe."

"It wasn't hard to figure out the combination. Grandma's birthday? Anyway I got the medical bag key out of your jacket pocket. There were so many interesting things to look at. Like the scalpels, the stethoscope, this little bottle of medicine…it's in my pocket…here, look."

"Oh no…"

"When I grow up I want to cut people open so I can look at their insides. What's it called?"

"Autopsies."
"Autopsies. That's what I want to do. So…I figured I would start to practice now, and I gave Mommy a shot."

"You…what?"

"I wanted to trick Mommy like the doctor tricks me. I practiced filling the needles from the little bottle early this morning in my room."

"Needles…?"

"Hey, you're sweating. Anyway, this morning Mommy was sitting on the bed, on the phone. When I went into her room, I hid her shot behind my back. After she hung up I pretended I wanted to hug her, and I stuck the needle into the side of her neck."

"You..."

"Oh, Uncle Edwin I was very careful. I took her organs out one at a time and made sure Mommy was good and healthy."

"No. God, no. This isn't a bug bite, is it?"

"Nope. I gave you your shot right there..."

# # #

Belinda Kimmons

Belinda Kimmons was born when rotary phones were still in use, and Superman could change in a phone booth. She retired after over twenty years as a civil servant. Since she retired, she spends hours ripping ideas out of her brain.

She has been writing something or other that was strange or creepy for a long time. Apparently the stories were creepy enough to invoke sufficient fear in one friend who admitted she was actually afraid to meet Belinda in person (which pleased her immensely). Writing was a hobby and she never considered publishing until her loving friends kicked her in several places with their collective boot.

The Fall

by **Vardan Partamyan**

His hand felt for a grip and found none. The downward slide continued unabated. There was no sense of movement as the total darkness stole all sense of time and motion. He was lost in nothingness where existence itself was a mere fictional category, along with all the other concepts that had already lost their meaning in his world – truth, freedom, hope… His world – what a naive statement, there was nothing his in that world that he helped create (or destroy - depending on your point of view and preference for over dramatization). It would be arrogant to suppose that he himself could have a lot to do with the way everything turned out. He was just your ordinary dictator from the eternal line of bureaucrats with clean hands and dirty conscience. After all, at the time, war seemed like a good idea, at least on paper. What wasn't in that five page memo, prepared by a whole flock of qualified experts, was the utter and irreversible destruction, death of about half of earth's population, total annihilation of human society as such and a nice little nuclear fallout that engulfed the world in a stylish grey fog that helped the surviving half of the humanity plunge into a further feat of self destruction against the ever engaging backdrop of burning cities…

Perhaps that particular nuclear disclaimer was in the appendix section of the report which he never cared to read. Another mystery that bothered him was less retrospective and more related to his present situation as he had absolutely no idea where he was and how he got there. His last memory was that of boarding a train, which ran deep under the ravaged capital of the country he once so diligently abused /served/ exploited/ governed/ misused/ destroyed. The train was to take him to the ever so promising "undisclosed safe location" from where he was to bring his unwavering voice of leadership to his people who undoubtedly needed wise words of advice/caution/empty promises/emotional addresses from their beloved ruler. Along for the ride on the three-carriage "train of hope" (for whom?) were the equally beloved members of the political/spiritual/intellectual/insert your pointless title here elite who were to guarantee the survival of the fittest (fattest).
Their descent into the tunnels went like a by-the-numbers military operation with the security personnel rushing them on through a

brightly lit staircase. The platoon commander reported that there was a risk of an external penetration by what he referred to as "unstable elements". The news was greeted by dismay from the high level refugees and especially their wives who, dressed up in their best fur coats, found the very idea of being on the run from their own humble servants utterly disturbing…

His memory faded for a moment and he was once again lost in his invisible descent. He couldn't say for sure but he had a feeling that he started to move faster. There was no wind, for all he knew there wasn't even air – just the sense of moving down, deeper and deeper. Then a brilliant idea occurred to him – he was just sleeping and going through one of those falling down nightmares. This idea brought immediate comfort. OK, all he needed to do now was to wake up. How about pinching himself awake? Sounds like a splendid idea! He reached out to do just that and froze. Something incomprehensible happened and his mind was simply refusing to accept it. This is just a dream - he tried telling himself but somehow knew better. The simple truth was that he couldn't pinch himself awake as he couldn't find his body. OK, calm down, there must be a logical (or illogical) explanation to this. Just need to think. Need to remember…

They were going down the stairs. They heard muffled cries and gunshots coming from above. The military said there was nothing to worry about. It seemed like the "unstable elements" had penetrated the premises of the government bunker, which contained the entrance to the underground depot. These people were mostly unarmed, the security said, and posed no immediate threat to the highly trained security personnel. Nevertheless, they were told to hurry up. He could see clear indications of panic in the lines of his supporters. Many people started running and, inevitably, one of the women, overburdened with the physical and financial sight effects of the good life, plunged down, dragging her elderly husband along for the ride. They tumbled down a flight and lay there. No one stopped - people just stepped over them and rushed on. He could hear the woman whining and the man cursing in his thin, cracked voice. The stairs went on and on and he witnessed two more similar accidents, which went along the same pattern. In a second, industrial giants and generals were reduced to slobbering creatures, begging for their life, trying to crawl, falling down again only to be succumbed by the ever louder screams of their hunters. Finally, they were at the train station… and there it was: the ticket out of this mess. The train with its gracious curves stood out as something ethereal in the otherwise dull surroundings of the depot. He paused for a second to appreciate it. Maybe it wasn't all lost after all? Maybe he would be able to get through this? So many times he was written off by his peers and time after time he had proven them wrong by finding and hanging on to the straw that would help him climb out of any ugly scandal. No "unstable element" would catch up to this baby! For the first time since the crisis (otherwise known as the end of the world) erupted, he was smiling. Once inside the train, his mood got even better – huge comfortable armchairs, drinks, glasses, soothing music – civilization! The gunshots and screams were closer than ever but he didn't worry. He felt that he had once again found that one tiny straw and he wasn't planning on letting it go…

His memories were once again interrupted as a new sensation entered his everlasting fall. He didn't understand the change at once but then a realization dawned on him – he was no longer in complete darkness. The pipe, and it was a pipe, he could see it for sure now, did have an end after all. Somewhere far below him, he could see a reddish glow. The surface of the pipe was not as smooth as he had initially thought – it was covered with strange signs and symbols. As they blurred by, he finally became aware of the speed of his fall. For a moment, he tried to concentrate on the light… that brought him right back to the train. All the passengers were already on board but for some reason the train was not moving. Outside, the soldiers were running around with their weapons drawn… there was a lot of shouting, occasional gunfire and one more sound. At first, he didn't recognize it and took it for the work of one of the engines of the train… But then he looked out… Out of the narrow exit of the stairway, hundreds of people were flooding out… the sound he heard was that of their feet hitting the concrete. Soldiers had passed on to full automatic fire. Their bullets cut through the advancing crowd. A small volcano of blood would erupt from someone's severed arm or leg. People would fall and immediately disappear in the rapidly advancing human wave.

Finally, the train started to move. He gave out a sigh of relief cut short by a shattering noise… he was showered with glass from the broken window. The train was gaining speed, the people on the platform flashed by like ghosts. He looked around but no one seemed to pay attention, not to the shattered window, not to the strange object next to him. All the passengers seemed to be in a semi daze: dethroned demigods braced to accept the new reality. He wanted to call someone but his throat was too dry and all that came out was an ugly hissing sound. Reluctantly, he reached down for the object - a small black box with a little red light blinking on the side. As he picked it up, the blinking became more rapid – the tiny red eye was winking at him, quicker, quicker, quicker… He felt that he couldn't make himself move, he was hypnotized by that tiny red spot that wanted to tell him something. Suddenly, the winking stopped and he was looking straight into the tiny red abyss…

The end of the pipe was getting closer. He could see its jagged edges. The red glow was stronger now… he could also feel the heat. As the realization dawned on him, he remembered an old Irish proverb: in life you only have two things to worry about: either you'll be healthy or you'll be ill. If you're healthy, you have nothing to worry about; if you're ill, you have only two things to worry about: either you'll get well or you'll die. If you get well, you have nothing to worry about, if you die, you have only two things to worry about: either you'll go to heaven or you'll go to hell. If you go to heaven, you have nothing to worry about and if you go to hell you'll be so busy shaking hands with old friends that you won't have any time to worry about anything. As the pipe ended, he saw (this is not possible) that he was in hell (so the descriptions are pretty accurate) and he sure didn't have any friends to shake hands with (plenty of enemies though)...

Time to worry…

# # #

Vardan Partamyan

Vardan Partamyan was born in Yerevan, Armenia, in 1983. After returning from studies in the US, he enrolled in the Yerevan State University - majoring in Political Science and English language. In the years that followed, he was an author of and contributor to a number of non-fiction publications mainly dealing with the issues and challenges facing his newly independent country. Writing fiction has been a long time passion/obsession for Vardan who mixes influences from writers such as Stephen King, J.R.R. Tolkien, Harry Harrison, Alfred Bester,

Ernest Hemingway and Ian Fleming with the eternal themes of a man's strive for freedom, the quest for self discovery and the knowledge of the unknown, presented on the backdrop of sometimes fantastical surroundings and events.

The Birthday Surprise: Preface
by Melvin B. Wylie Jr

It's your birthday, and you're alone at home, and you receive a package from UPS. You place the box on your table and open it wondering what is inside. When you open the box you find the following items:

1) A lot of money bundled in one-hundred dollar bills wrapped neatly in a vacuum sealed pouch.
2) A small guillotine.
3) A smaller box with return postage. Inside the little box is zip lock baggie.
4) A letter addressed to you.

The letter reads

Happy Birthday!

The $100,000,000.00 is for you to keep!

But there is a catch. I know the contents of the box are quite confusing, but as they say, nothing is free, there is always a price.

The guillotine is for your fingers. You read right. Whichever hand you write with, you must cut off your thumb and ring finger. This is not a joke. If you have broken the seal to the money you have already taken the first step and a price must be paid. If you have not broken the seal then good for you! You still have some choices.

Once the seal to the money bag is broken, you must begin cutting. The guillotine is spring loaded so it will be quick and painful. You cannot go to the hospital, and you cannot tell anyone why you severed your fingers. This secret is between you and I. If you do say I will know and within the next three days you will be captured and slowly cut apart piece by piece. I assure you it will be a painful death. Once the chosen finger and thumb is cut off you must place them in the ziplock bag, then into the small box and drop it in the mail using the return address. That's it! It's so easy to enjoy the $100,000,000.00

Think of what you can do with all the money! How better off you and your family will be. But always remember this contract is bound from the time you opened the box. No telling!

But don't jump for joy yet! If you have not broken the seal then these are your choices:
Do nothing. That's right you can do nothing and lose the $100,000,000. Place the box with all its contents outside your door and someone will be by to pick it up. But there is also a price for doing nothing. If you choose to do nothing, the same package will be delivered to a close loved one will receive it on their birthday. Of course, they will have the same choices as you.

Now don't start running and warning your loved ones about this package otherwise the people you tell will start mysteriously dying. This goes for ANYONE you tell. Now you don't want that on your conscience do you?
Here is another choice. I know this may be a hard decision so keep the box for 24 hours and think about it. At the end of 24 hours, a decision must be made. If you hold the box past 24 hours, you will reach an untimely but peaceful death.

Happy Birthday my friend! Have fun.

What would you do? Nonetheless, I'll see you on your birthday.

Melvin B. Wylie Jr

Melvin is a happily married father of 7 children living in the Washington DC area. An active environmentalist who interviews people from across the globe about sustainability and humanitarian issues. Currently working at The George Washington University in a number of Facilities Management and Event Support Positions. Enjoys writing about and an avid reader of science fiction and horror stories. "This is an introduction to a book I am writing based on 'The Birthday Surprise'.

List of Authors

Aaron Valla
Belinda Kimmons
Daniel Kaye
Greg Hair
Lily Margaret Howlett
Luke Peter Mepham
P.L. DuPee
Jason .R. Lloyd
James G. Kelly
Peter Hartke
Richard Lague Jr
Robert A. Read
Ruhaani
Saul Hudson
Stephanie Ayers
Todd Martin
Vardan Partamyan
Wally Holderness
Melvin B. Wylie Jr

Share your Feedback with us!

We are always interested in getting your feedback and find what interests you more, so reach out to us through your comments and suggestions at jagrit@shortnscarystories.com